JONATHAN'S VENTURE

WAI KIT CHIANG

LitPrime
"Your story is our priority"

LitPrime Solutions
21250 Hawthorne Blvd
Suite 500, Torrance, CA 90503
www.litprime.com
Phone: 1 (209) 788-3500

Published by LitPrime Solutions   02/04/2021

ISBN: 978-1-953397-73-7(sc)
ISBN: 978-1-953397-74-4(e)

Library of Congress Control Number: 2021902253

TABLE OF CONTENTS

Every student new to the college must take a class in 'Orientation' on his first semester at the college. In the 'Orientation Class', the new student will be introduced to the college and what the college can provide. He will be provided with information on the majors and courses that will be available to him, the facilities that will be available to him for his studies, and the resources that will be available on campus and off campus. The students are encouraged to choose their major and classes wisely, and use all the facilities and resources productively.

The journal 'Jonathan's Venture' is an orientation to introduce the reader to the mechanics of non-organic autonomy, the mechanics of bio-organic autonomy, and the mechanics of social autonomy. This journal will give only a brief perspective on these subjects. Hypotheses and speculations to it will be brought up in different places on the journal to encourage the reader to search further on the subject(s) that bring interest to the mind. The reader is encouraged to prove the speculations and share what he has found.

This Journal is dedicated to my late brother, Wai Ning
Chiang. Wai Ning Chiang was born on 27 July 1967.
He passed away on 27 Oct. 1987 from Leukemia.

I give my acknowledgments to the researchers and authors
of the resources used in constructing this journal.

INTRODUCTION: REMINISCENCE OF THE VENTURES

A commercial space craft is leaving the lower orbit of Earth heading toward a station in a higher orbit. As the craft is gliding toward the station, a passenger is looking out of his window and reminiscing about the history of traveling vessels man has built and the journeys he has made.

Commander Robert Jameson sees a small one man boat traveling along the coast of an island. The passenger is fishing.

He then sees a large ship that is about to leave port. Man is no longer just traveling on one man vessels. A vessel this size will require a staff of several personnel present to manage and operate her. Each person will be assigned to a specific duty to manage and operate the vessel.

The crew of the vessel forms a republic of personnel that is maintained under a chain of command. The seamen are assigned to specific duties in a specific area. Each area of duty will be maintained under the command of a senior officer. The senior officer or executives of a department will work together under a commanding officer, namely the captain. They will provide advice to the captain in accordance with their particular area qualifications. The captain will abide by charter and directives under which he serves and give commands accordingly.

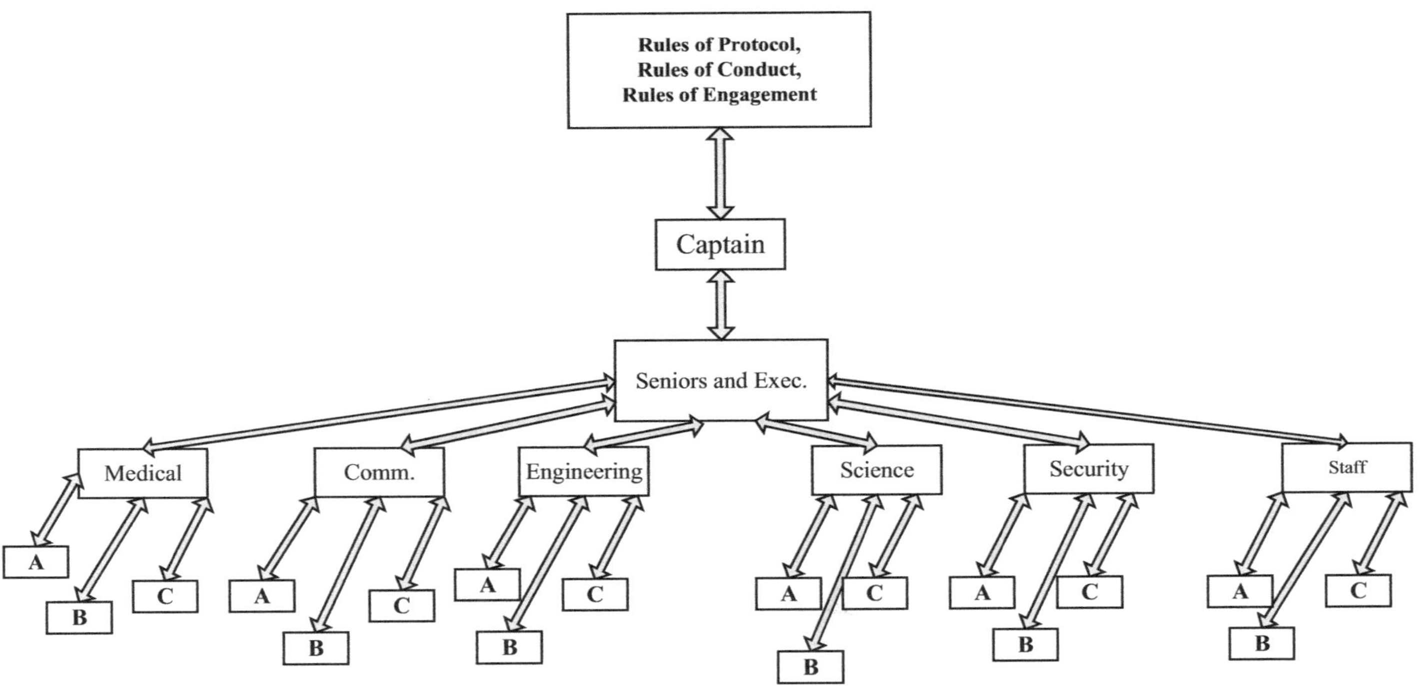

Rules of Protocol, Rules of Conduct, Rules of Engagement
Captain
Seniors and Exec.
Medical
A
B
C
Comm.
A
B
C
Engineering
A
B
C
Science
A
B
C
Security
A
B
C
Staff
A
B
C

After pondering the evolution of sea vessels, Commander Jameson begins to take notice of man's journeys in the sky. He sees a small one man aircraft. He then sees a larger aircraft consisting of a pilot, a co-pilot, a navigator, and several attendants. This large aircraft operates using the system like the old sea ships.

Man learned to travel into the sky.

He now travels into space.

Sea and air, along with land, were once divided into 4 branches of service. When man became united together in their journeys into space, the 4 branches are united into 1 branch.

THE JOURNEY BEGINS

REMINISCING JONATHAN

After docking with space station Alpha, Commander Jameson passes through quarantine and heads directly toward the director's office. As he walks, the commander considers his career as an officer in United Federation's space program. He received his promotion a mere 3 years after graduating from the Space Academy; then serving as a test pilot - flying new aircrafts for speed and distance, and finally training for the space program.

After 3 years in piloting duty, Ensign Robert Jameson was promoted to Commander Jameson and assigned to duty on board the space ship the UFS Alpha. He was greeted by Captain Jonathan to serve as his executive officer in serving as the administrator in charge of the internal affairs on board the UFS Alpha. During the 15 years of his administrative duties on board the UFS Alpha, Commander Jameson received direct experience in republic order on board a traveling vessel that would be out of port and civilization for long periods of time.

After 15 years on board the UFS Alpha, Robert Jameson received his well earned 2 year leave. 8 months into his leave, 2 officers came to his private vacation home on a remote island far from civilization with written instructions for him to return to duty immediately. As 2 officers escort Commander Jameson back to base to his assignment, the commander wonders, "Why am I suddenly being called back to duty? What is so important that they have to send 2 officers to my home to escort me directly to my assignment?"

As he approaches the director's office, Commander Jameson looks out the window and takes notice of a craft under construction. "They have finally approved of my proposal for a large space vessel that will need more than just pilot(s), navigator(s), and a small crew of senior officers."

The director then comes out of his office and greets Commander Jameson.

"Welcome Robert. How was your trip to Alpha? I'm sorry for having to disturb you from your long awaited leave. The United Federation Space Program has been working on a long voyage project for some time. We've come up with a new type of engine that can provide much power for long distance thrust; for long space travel out of hibernation; and a new hull design that will enable the mass explorations. The only thing we need now is a crew and a commander. Your proposal for the Earth Space Program to sponsor long exploration travels with the crew not placed in hibernation shows us that you are aware of how this long exploration journey must be carried out. We have been waiting for you 'Captain Jameson'."

"This new prototype space vessel has been designed and the outer surface of its hull is near completion. We now have to construct the internal networks and departments of this vessel. The crew that will have to live in this travelling home must be familiar with it and be able to repair and modify it during their journey. The UFS Jonathan (the United Federation Ship Jonathan) is yours. We want you to hand pick the best people for your crew. They must be able to live with each other and work with each other comfortably. You and your crew must participate in the final construction of the Jonathan so you can become familiar with the vessel to the final details and will be confident on how to do any modifications on her."

Conception and Construction

Man has learned to travel from the local orbit around planet Earth to the outer orbit of the solar system. Local porting stations and outer porting stations have been built. It's time to travel beyond the local solar system and start studying and researching the local galaxy and beyond. These ventures will be of great distances at long periods of time. This will be done with great speed; speed by distance not how fast. Proper power source and structural design will be required for the great distances. Proper provisions, crew and social psychology will be required for the long periods of time the crew will be from civilization. The crew in this lone vessel will be their sole civilization.

Last known source of power was solar. Solar will be natural and will need the sun. There will be points where there will be no source of sun light. Battery reserve through molten salt will not last long. Means to extract sun and store battery reserve will take up much space making the vessel awkward. After a period of time, man had found a new way of creating much power from small amounts of energy source and matter. A new way of producing great stores of energy (power) from directing a small pulse of energy toward a contained matter has been found. A new way of containing massively produced power that also produces nuclear effects have been found. A power plant that produces this power can be built into a large vessel.

A new means of producing much power (great stores of energy) will enable a massively built sophisticated space vessel to run efficiently for long periods of time. A Matrix of large and well protected tubes will carry ionic compounds to provide mass amounts of energy source (stores of energy, power) to many areas at fast timing. Molten salt is liquid at normal temperature level. It can be ionized to such quality to enable the liquid to have organic qualities; this organic liquid compound will respond to energy stimuli to reproduce and develop new molecular-cellular packs to carry and move stores of energy in packs. The molecular-cellular packs will respond fast and reproducing quickly. Each pack will carry large stores of energy.

A second power engine will be present in the vessel. This second engine will not be as large or as powerful as the first engine that produces great power from energy pulses into the contained matter. This second engine will direct the produced power into the ionized liquid compound. Organic packs will be produced to carry large amounts of energy down the tube to the areas in need and use of the power and stores of energy. The second engine will produce the 1st pack; then produces the 2nd pack. The second pack will provide the energy for the 1st pack to produce a pack. The engine will add stores of energy and power onto the pack it stimulates in reproduction. As the pack stimulates the pack ahead of it to reproduce another pack, it also adds stores of energy to the pack reproduced. A store of energy will be entered on the pack created ahead of it. The delivery of the store of energy will be as fast as the packs are being produced ahead of it. A large vessel with much power and is well energized can be built for long voyages.

Space vessels have been built only for short distances (distances within the solar system only) have a long stem-hull with compartment(s) rotating around the stem-hull for virtual gravitational force in the compartment. A vessel with compartments rotating around a long stem-hull makes the vessel awkward. In the vacuum of space, there will be no worries of counter force during the motion; but there will be difficulty in maneuvering. Every area in the vessel, the stem-hull and the compartment, must have propulsion holes to enable proper maneuver. Impulse holes all over one tight object in the vacuum of space will make maneuvering easy. A disorganized object with motions of compartments along the stem hull of the vessel will make the coordinated maneuver long and awkward. The surface structure of this object is unorganized. The disorganization will be a nuisance in coordinating and agile maneuver. It will have weaponry for defense; but its true defense should be its energy shield around the vessel and the vessel's agility.

This prototype vessel will glide through the vacuum of space in hyper space. A pathway will be created by this vessel to travel to its target at hyper speed (hyper space in a short path to target). The pathway created by the tight vessel object is only for this tight vessel object. The helmsman-navigator must create a smooth path toward the target (great distance or a very short distance) before riding onto the pathway to the target. The hyper space is in a hyper pathway (hyper tunnel) that is constantly built as the vessel travels. The agility of the vessel will enable this vessel to travel through the vacuum of space smoothly. While inside the hyper space, the tight vessel will move or not move and will still be protected by wall around the vessel's hyperspace.

The Jonathan will become part of the energy tunnel; energy beam to target. The tunnel created will bring the target point to the vessel. In a moment of time a step will be taken. The tunnel will enable the vessel to reach a great distance in that moment the single walk step is taken. A great distance will have been travelled in that moment of time; how the Jonathan has traveled will no longer be in speed but in distance, and dimension, through the strength of the tunnel.

The new power production and new means of energizing (energy conduction) can produce virtual gravitational force for the inner hull and an energy shield around the hull. This large vessel can be one tight object body instead of a long large object. One tight object can ride along an energy path it creates with less difficulty than a long object. Areas for power production, provisions, bridge control, crew quarters, resting lounge(s) and gardens can be in one tight object body with little difficulty in travel in the vessel. The provision area will provide storage for clothing and mechanical supplies. Natural food supplement, water and oxygen will be provided by the large garden(s). This is going to be a long research voyage and diplomatic voyage so food will have to be produced on board the vessel. Water and oxygen will be produced from the plants and the energy from the vessel. Propulsion holes will be all around the tight vessel; but maneuverability will be easy with much agility. The differences in propulsion at different areas will not have to be much.

The UFS Jonathan is a tight and hollow object in space. There will be impulse holes around the vessel to enable all motion in the vacuum of space. There will be three walls around the vessel. The inner wall is metallic and will hold a virtual gravitational force inside the vessel. It will maintain the gravitational force for the living environment to house the crew and the garden. The outer wall is a non solid energy field that protects the vessel in its hyperspace barrier from external encounters. Every object will have its own hyperspace dimension and barrier. There will be a thick metal wall between the inner wall and the outer wall. This thick wall is the shell of the hull and will hold the entire vessel together.

A robot is a machine that can operate on its own to do tasks it has been instructed to. An android operates the way it has been programmed to. It can only do as much as its parts are permitted to. A drone is as sophisticated as a robot but it is controlled by self-aware user and operator of the machine. The drone can do things it was not previously programmed to do at the last moment, at the control of the user. The UFS Jonathan is a drone vessel with the user-controller at the bridge.

The Jonathan is a sophisticated robot. Every plate on the vessel is a cellular point in a mass cybernetic network. The central network control at the bridge of the Jonathan is so advance in consciousness and intelligence that it can monitor every cellular point, control every part of the vessel, and relay all information to the crew and officers. The UFS Jonathan is a prototype. There has been no known space vessel that can monitor itself and control itself and serve along with the crew and officers as a member of the crew.

Each area on the vessel will have a station that monitors all the cellular points in the area. The different areas will relay all their information to the central network control. Every point, every area, and the network control will operate automatically as they were programmed to. Each station will work with a crew member present to give last minute control alterations. If there is no crew member present, the station at the location will operate automatically as programmed to but will be monitored and controlled by the CNC at the bridge. The CNC of the Jonathan, will work with the bridge officer(s) to make the final request and command on how something shall be done. If there is no officer(s) present to give any final command, the CNC of the Jonathan will make the commands as it was trained (learned) and programmed to.

A 2nd matrix line will also pass through the 2nd Engine. The 2nd matrix line will contain ionized gas to deliver energized communication signals through the vessel. The ionized gaseous organic packs (molecular-cellular packs in ionized gas similar to cellular packs in the ionized liquids) will be constructed by the 2nd Engine the same way the ionized liquid organic packs are in the 1st engine. The procedure in delivering energy and message signals through the ionized gaseous packs will be the same way as delivering power through the ionized liquid packs.

Energy level through the ionized liquid line will cause reflexive reaction amongst the motor areas. Specific energy levels and quantities of the energy levels will give specific signals for specific actions according to that stations programming. The reception and response will send message signals by quantity and quality level of energy to the CNC at the bridge. The bridge will automatically or manually respond with instructions to the rest of the vessel.

The quantum matrix forms a barrier around the ship forming a dimension and environment in the ship. The quantum matrix forms a tunnel for the ship to travel a great distance in a brief amount of seconds. No matter how far the ship has travelled in space, the amount of seconds passed in the ship will be the same amount of seconds passed on Earth.

The Crew and Protocol

This will be large vessel for research and exploration. There will be an executive officer to manage the internal affairs of the ship, an engineering officer, a communication officer, a medical officer, a science officer, security officer and social-psychologist; the senior officers. The ship will also have experienced engineers, experienced communication experts, experienced physicians and medical assistants, and experts in sociology, archeology, anthropology, technology, etc.

Since this is a prototype vessel, all members of the crew must participate in the construction of the vessel. The engineering officer and his team must participate in the construction of the power production system. The members of the engineering department and the technical experts will have to participate in the aligning of the energizing matrix. Since this ship (the vessel and its crew) will be making long journeys, everyone must go through psychological training and physical & medical preparation.

The commander of UFS Jonathan, Captain Jameson, will command and represent UFS Jonathan as a whole. He will take advises from his senior officers, and learn about the ships condition from reports by the senior officers. The members of each department will report to the senior officer that is responsible for that department. The senior officer responsible for the department will report the situation to the captain, and share information with fellow senior officers to determine how to work with them in maintaining the ship and carrying out the duty of the mission.

The Commander:	Captain Robert Jameson;
Executive Officer:	Commander Richard Johns;
Medical Officer:	Commander James Carl;
Communication Officer:	Lt. Commander Thomas James;
Engineering Officer:	Lt. Commander Katherine Mat;
Science Officer:	Lt. Commander Joan Kevin;
Security Officer:	Lt. Commander Terry Xiao;
Inventory Officer & Staff Officer;	Lt. Junior Grade Terry Mans.
Counselor	Lt. Commander Sheryl Simmons

Captain Jameson will work with Jonathan (the CNC of the UFS Jonathan) and the rest of the ship to confront the external encounters during their ventures. Commander Johns will work with Jonathan, the CNC of Jonathan, along with his fellow seniors to know and control the internal operations of the entire ship (the crew and the vessel). Commander Carl will work with the CNC and the crew to deal with the bio-physical condition the crew is in and how the environment will affect the crew. Lt. Commander James will work with the CNC and his staff to monitor and control the internal communications connection (audio, visual, and computer) on board the vessel and the communication connections made outside of the vessel. Lt. Commander Mat works with Jonathan (the CNC) and her staff to monitor and control all power connections and mechanical operations on board the vessel. Lt. Commander Kevin will work with the CNC and her staff on the scientific research and conditions the Jonathan will encounter during their ventures. Lt. Commander Xiao will work with the CNC and her staff to police the vessel and ensure security and defense externally. Lt. Mans will work with the CNC, the senior officers and the rest of the crew to handle the environment on board the vessel, the inventory and supply, the botanical garden station to provide food and needs while on the ventures, and the regular work schedule of the crew. Cmd. Simmons will work with the CNC archive and each person's present situation to determine the crew member's psychological condition. She will also work with the CNC and the vessel's communication system to determine the social psychological condition of the intelligence the UFS Jonathan encounters.

Each crew member must be a specialist in one field to be assigned toward a specific department and area of operation. Each member must also be knowledgeable in other fields so they can assist in other areas and departments if he must be temporarily assigned to other areas to provide assistance when needed. Since this is a research vessel, all crew members must be knowledgeable in education and diplomacy. They must be able to share knowledge of their specific fields diplomatically amongst each other and with any guests outside of their diplomatic research vessel.

Each senior officer and crew member will participate in the construction of the UFS Jonathan. Each crew member will participate in the construction while the Jonathan is in the 'womb'; while the Jonathan is in the dry-dock port at the Alpha space station. Until the Jonathan is completely constructed and fully operational, the Jonathan will not be commissioned and come to life.

The crew will have to become vegetarians and consume food supplement from the plants grown in the garden(s). It will be unhygienic and unwise to have animal farms on board the vessel. There will not be enough room for processed meat provisions for the long voyage. The crew will have to accept what the vessel can provide.

The Commission

The vessel is completed. All members of the crew to serve on board the UFS Jonathan have gone through training and learned every detail of the vessel and its communication and power linings during construction and fitting. All areas of the vessel have gone through testing. All adjustments required have been made. Further adjustments for the journeys will be made during the journeys. The crew will be divided in ranks, duties and positions by their skills and performances, not favoritism. The crew will learn to live together and trust their lives with each other.

The UFS Jonathan and its crew can now be commissioned and begin its exploration beyond this solar system.

NON-BIO-ORGANIC AUTONOMY

THE BUILDING BLOCK OF A VESSEL AND DEVICE

A mass autonomous mechanical object consists of many sub-autonomous mechanical objects. Autonomous mechanical objects are matter objects that are constructed of autonomies and sub-autonomies. A matter object is the autonomy of sub-particles called molecules. A molecule is the autonomy of different atoms of different elements. The sub-atomic particles (the neutrons, protons, and electrons) will determine how the atom of the element will relate with other elements to form the autonomy of the molecule and how the atoms, the molecule(s) and the matter object will perform (take affect with other matter objects and their atomic particles).

A computer is a device that is constructed of many smaller devices along with wirings to link them together. The elements in the molecules determine how the devices and wires will be constructed and how they will perform along with each other. The quality of performance of this device will be determined by its sub-devices and sub-particles. Just as the computer device is determined by its sub-devices and sub-particles, so are all other autonomous mechanical objects, other autonomous matter objects.

Conception is creating what does not yet exist. Creating a matter object will be determined by the sub-atom of elements and molecules that will be used in constructing this object. The sub-atomic design of the element will be the generic map (genetic map) of the matter object. Elements will be present. Elements capable of joining with each other and working with each other will determine the molecule(s) that form one of the parts of the matter object or mechanism/device/organ. The chemical/molecules of the organism(s) will determine how they work with each other and how the full matter object will be constructed, evolved and operated.

The building block and generic design of the matter object

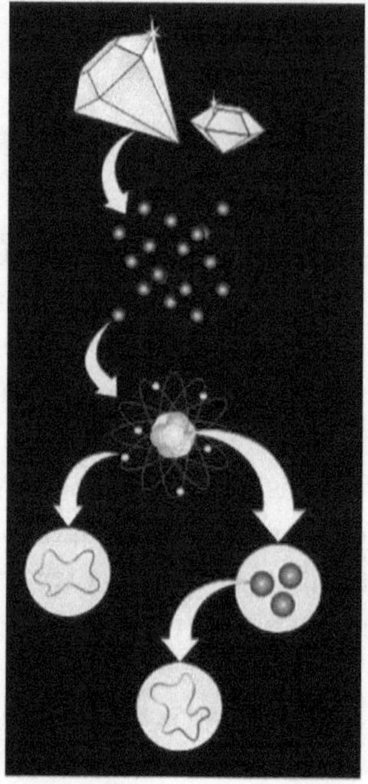

Fig. 1[1]

The mathematical formulations form the strings of the nodes of the quarks. The amounts of the nodes of quarks form the neutrons, protons and electrons present in the element. The amount of protons and electrons present in the element determines the formation of the molecule. The molecule(s) in the object will determine how the matter object will evolve and perform.

The building block and generic design of the power line

Energy is force delivered a distance to a place where work will be done. Impulse is momentum/motion of matter to a distance to do work. Power

---

[1] Wikipedia (2011), String Theory, http://en.wikipedia.org/wiki/String_Theory

is a store of energy for work to be done. Fuel is source of power (store of energy) and source of matter. Energy enables momentum and impulse.

A fuel line consists of matter object(s) that enable the delivery of power to areas for energy to do work. The generic design of the molecule by the generic designs of the elements will determine how the elements and molecules will work together and form the matter object. This will eventually determine how the matter object (mechanism or organism) will operate. The wire lines to be constructed, being constructed, are determined by the generic design of the contents in the wiring and the generic design of the fuel and power source that will travel through the lines. The wirings will evolve and be constructed along the generic design of the structure and the generic design of the content for which the structure has been built.

The amount of the content traveling through the power line built will affect the entire autonomy of the structure the power line is in. The devices that are linked to the power line and use the power delivered to it affect the overall operation and performance of the entire structure.

The building block and generic design of the communication network

A complex structure consisting of many internal devices and parts must link all the parts together. All must work in coordination to maintain the autonomy of the structure. As a matrix of power lines connect all devices together to provide power to all, a matrix of communication lines must be present to enable all the devices to 'talk' with each other so all will work together and ensure autonomy in the complex device, matter object.

The generic design of the sub-atom, the atom, and the molecules are the map of the structural body, not the map and 'character' of the administrator operating and directing the autonomous body. The devices/mechanisms inside the matter object form the autonomy of the object. The autonomy is the object. The more elements present to construct the molecule, the more complex the molecule. The more mechanisms present to operate the autonomous device, the more complex this mass structure is. The mechanisms will have to do much work while maintaining autonomy; the work of transferring power to each other, of communicating with each other and coordinating with each other.

DISTRIBUTION OF POWER AND RESOURCE

The android physiology simulates the anatomy/autonomy of a bio-organic body. An android consists of many computer stations to operate specific responsibilities. Each work station and each motor area in the android's body will require power and energy to operate and do the work it is there to do. Power will be distributed by the android's internal body to feed the individual stations and motor areas.

'Raw' resources, solar, nuclear, bio-, etc. will enter into the android body. The body will consume (accept and use) the resources to produce the fuel and power it needs. There is a motor area and mechanism that will refine the raw resource to the type of power the body's mechanisms use. Fuel provides the energy and matter to be used. Each motor area and mechanism has its purpose in maintaining the autonomous body of the android. The motor mechanism will take in the refined fuel and energy source and use it to operate the area. The mechanism will trigger impulses in the fuel and energy source as it operates and develops.

As power and energy travel from mechanism to mechanism and do work, its capacity/quality drops. The work done on a mechanism will enhance the mechanism's capacity to amplify the momentum and impulse in the fuel (power source) that is passing on from this mechanism. As the impulse amplifies, the mechanisms will develop and improve in operation.

Pythagorean Theorem

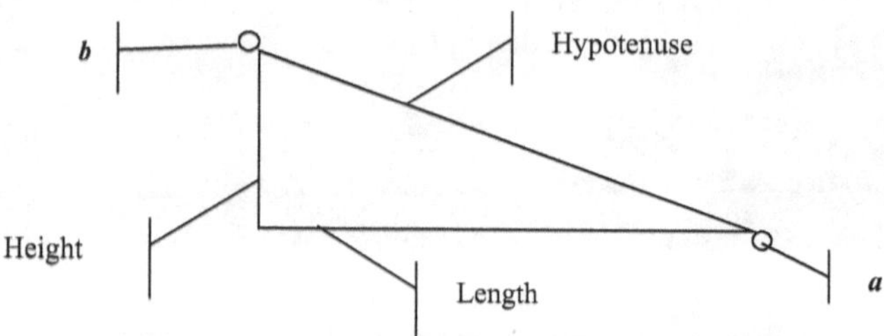

> Hypotenuse^2 = Length^2 + Height^2;
> Hypotenuse and Length meets at point *a*, and Hypotenuse and Height meets at point *b*;
> The triangle will spin around center point *a*;
> The Hypotenuse of the triangle is the radius *(R)* and distance from center point *a* to point *b* at the circumference perimeter;
> Each degree in the circumference is a dimension;
> There are 360 dimensions in a circumference, and 360^2 degrees in a sphere;
> Whatever degree and dimension the triangle is in, the radius *(R)* (Hypotenuse) will always be the same.

Energy

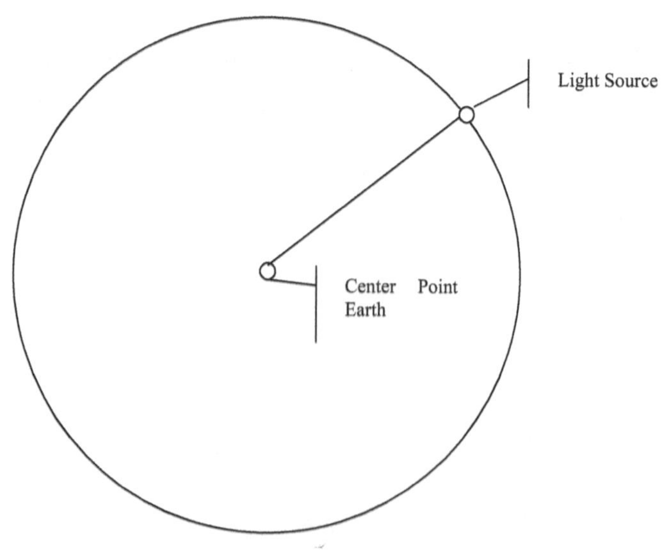

___Matter is Energy; Energy is Matter:___
___Matter is a different form of Energy as Energy is a different form of___
___Matter:___
$E = mc2;$
$E = Fc * R;$ [2]
$E = (m * v2/R) * R;$ [3]
$E = mv2; v = c;$
$E = mc2.$

Energy varies as momentum of light varies[4,5]

Neutrino[6] is a neutral sub-atomic energy particle with no electrical charge. The String Theory is mathematical formulation recognizing energy that

---

[2] Fc is centripetal force; $Fc = mv2 / R.$

The light source is in motion. Earth is the center point observing the light source in motion. As the light source rotates, the center point stays in the same position; the light source is in a circular path. Visual distance from the center point to the light source in circular motion is R.

R = radius from the light source on the circumference around Earth to the center point Earth.

c is the speed of light; $v = c.$

Energy is the store of force delivering particle(s) of neutrino(s) to cause visual effect on the observer at the center point. No matter what the distance of R is, it is the store of force that is being measured.

[3] Energy is the store of force that enables an object particle to move in circular path. The store of force is delivered the distance of R; from the rotating force in the circumference, circular path, of the object in motion to enable the object to move at the speed of light.

By centripetal force, distance from where the force of the mass begins to where the force of the mass will confront the situation and do work that is the radius of the circumference, R.

Energy is delivery of force (momentum of organized mass; effort) to a distance to confront the situation (to do work; cause effect on the target).

[4] **Live**Science (22 Sept. 2011), Particles May Travel Faster than Light, Breaking Laws of Physics. http://news.yahoo.com/strange-particles-may-travel-faster-light-breaking-laws-192010201.html.

[5] ABCNews Science (23 Sept. 2011), Neutrino Faster Than Light Maybe. Revising Relativity, http://abcnews.go.com/blogs/technology/2011/09/neutrino-faster-than-light-maybe/.

[6] Wikipedia (October 2011), Neutrino, http://en.wikipedia.org/wiki/Neutrino#Mass.

forms the quarks in quantum physics. Neutrino passes through elementary mass particles. The neutrino particle joins electrons forming Leptons[7]. It affects the quarks in quantum space and mechanics. The qualities and quantities of sub-atomic particles known as neutrons, protons and electrons are determined by the nodes/quarks. The sub-atomic particles determine how the atoms of different elements and particles will construct molecules constructing the objects that are used.

Neutrino can pass through standardized particles because it is neutral to positive or negative electro-magnetic energy (protons and electrons of the particle). Neutrinos are produced from radioactive decay. There are 3 generations of neutrinos. The different generations of neutrinos and different quantities of the neutrinos will manipulate matter, energy and the environment; and vice versa. Different environments will bring different results, different effects and different reactions for the same quantity of the same elementary mass particle.

Quantum is the small amount of an element's minute subatomic particles. These minute particles are particles of energy and are not recognized (measured) as atomic or subatomic mass particles; but are measures of string waves (measures/amounts of neutrinos). Neutrinos become a signal. The amount of neutrinos and leptons will manipulate the formation of mass will become a signal to the mass, energy and environment on how they will react.

Energy was and is determined by the speed of light and the mass that will be doing work a distance away in an amount of time. The environment will affect the quantity and quality of the energy particle and its momentum. The distance a mass or particle traveled in an amount of time varies in different environments. The momentum of the speed of light is no longer constant but measured as a variable. The strength and power of the energy produced by the mass provided will be determined by the environment the mass is held in and produced in.

The primary generator will collect the raw resources to produce the required power the autonomous body will need and use. This generator will produce

---

[7] Wikipedia, Lepton. http://en.wikipedia.org/wiki/Lepton

power supply, the source of energy and the matter, for the work stations and motor areas to use. If the power supply is too rich and strong, that administrator of this body must find a means to incorporate the power, or the body will be damaged. If the power supply produced is poor and not strong enough, the stations and motor areas will have difficulty(s) operating. Operation will be slow waiting for the power supply to build up.

The more work to be done, the more power needed and used. If there is not enough power, energy source and matter, the network or work stations, motor areas, and the power line will begin slowing down to the point of suspension and eventually shutting down. If anything shuts down, it will take time to restore to full function. The body will not be at full capacity until its entire network is fully functional (parts restored or replaced).

Power distribution

Power lines are linked from work station to work station. A work station will require energy source and matter to do work. As the fuel travels from station to station, its capacity begins to diminish. In the process of using the power received for motor work, the diminishing power is also being refined (enhanced/amplified in impulse momentum) to provide the type of power the other stations will require.

Resource distribution

A matrix of power lines connecting station with station formulates autonomy of the mechanical body. Power circulates from station to station, from area to area, in the matrix of power lines. As the fuel delivers the energy to do work, the fuel also delivers a mass of matter to be used by the motor station to build on and enhance the fuel and power. As the outer body develops to adapt the circumstances, the motor must develop along. The mass of matter provided by the fuel and power are used by the motor station to build on.

Usage of power and resource

Whatever type of power or fuel that the body has created from the raw resources in the external, the body will always use this type. The type of fuel (power source) will always be the same but the amount of power (power levels) will differ at different work stations and motor areas. The different power levels will deliver different amounts or different types of masses of matters for different areas to develop and operate by. Different level of energy will be in different masses of matter traveling at different level of impulses.

> - Primary generator refines the raw resources.
> - Specific power level carrying different levels of energy and different quantities of matter to specific work stations and different motor areas will be giving instructions for specific operation.
> - Instructions will be different levels of impulses leading to different reflexive responses.
> - Specific areas will learn to operate in accordance to the different power levels delivered to it in specific situations.
> - The different power levels and different amounts of matter will be used to develop the motor areas, work stations, and the body.

As the model of the android body becomes more complex, the amount of work stations and motor areas increase in amount. In the increase of motor areas and work stations, the matrix of power lines becomes more complex and sophisticated. The motor operations become more complex. The power supply, energy source and supply of matter, must keep circulating through the matrix of power line. The autonomous body must keep in motion to have the power supply circulating, used and enhanced. The energy is by impulse. Circulation is impulse momentum. The motion of the autonomous body will have all stations and motor areas performing/enhancing the impulse for developing reaction.

Power provides energy and action that enables work to be done. Impulse of matter and quantity/quality of energy is power enabling work to be done by the stations and the motor areas.

JOINT EFFORT OF POWER, BODY AND OPERATION BY THE COMMUNICATION NETWORK

The autonomous android body consists of a matrix of work stations and motor areas. They are linked to each other by a network of power lines. The power lines deliver fuel (power source) and energy. The autonomous body uses the same type of power all over the body, but at different levels for different motor areas and different operations. Signals of instructions will be delivered and interpreted by different work stations for specific purposes. The motor area will react by reflexive response toward the physical message brought about by the physical mass transported through the power line by impulse.

Construction of the matrix

The mass of matter and energy source (power) only gives a simple instruction through impulses. The simple instruction will be reacted to by reflexive response the motor area is trained through time and repeated drills. Detailed messages will be delivered to the motor area to give more detailed instructions for actions and reactions that were never prepared for. New information gathered at the motor area by audio, visual, and/ or somatic sensory will be directed to the central network control to be processed and evaluated. The central network control (traffic center of the communication signals) will then decide if the situation can be responded to automatically or not according to previous training through experiences and evaluation. If it is something new, the results will be delivered to the administrator and mind of the central network control and the controller and resident of this autonomous body. The detailed messages, beyond power delivery, are electrical-cybernetic signals in a cybernetic network.

Control of body by processing the communication network

The central control will give detailed messages to the specific areas. The CNC is the 'traffic control' that will relay communication signals to specific areas intended. The message(s) will be delivered through a communication line that is built along the path way of the power line, but on a separate line. The message will be delivered in impulses of energy packets. A message will be broken down to different quantities/qualities of energy packets (bytes). The message will prepare the recipient(s) of the message to receive the completion of the cybernetic message and respond to it immediately. The mechanism that received the cybernetic signal will direct its position. This will affect the impulse preparing the mechanism for later impulses. The message may have to be broken down and sent to different areas for different performances. The message will give different areas instruction to perform differently but in coordination to each other.

Universal physics and mechanics will give instructions for automated response, reflexive reaction. Detailed messages to give and receive messages go through a communication line, not the power line. Signals of broken messages will jump from station to station in the communication line. Each station will amplify or strengthen the signal by enhancing the diminishing energy load used in the communication line.

Control of network by the central network

The central network control is a powerful motor area that consists of many sophisticated stations, and towers that process specific data. Each station here is large to store much files and data, and is able to process new data and relate them with old data to refine old data files or construct new files. The new data will be received, processed, filed and used as the station has been previously prepared or preprogrammed to.

Each tower will be responsible for many work stations and will have many outlets for specific areas. To receive data and process them, outlets in the tower will be linked to each other. The linkage of outlets of the tower will appear like a spaghetti mess. Communication lines will link towers together to share processed data for central processing. The lines are entangled like a spaghetti mess.

However ugly the entanglements may appear to be, this area is fully capable in monitoring and maintaining order in the complex autonomy of motor areas, work stations, power lines, and communication lines. The lines will be constructed by the amount of matter and the amount of energy it has been provided with. The architecture of the line will be constructed according to the generic design of the element's atom and the molecule(s) that is formed by the organization of the atoms. Should anything happen, detour arrangements will be constructed in accordance to the elements of the surrounding environment, matter available and the power available.

Mechanical Network

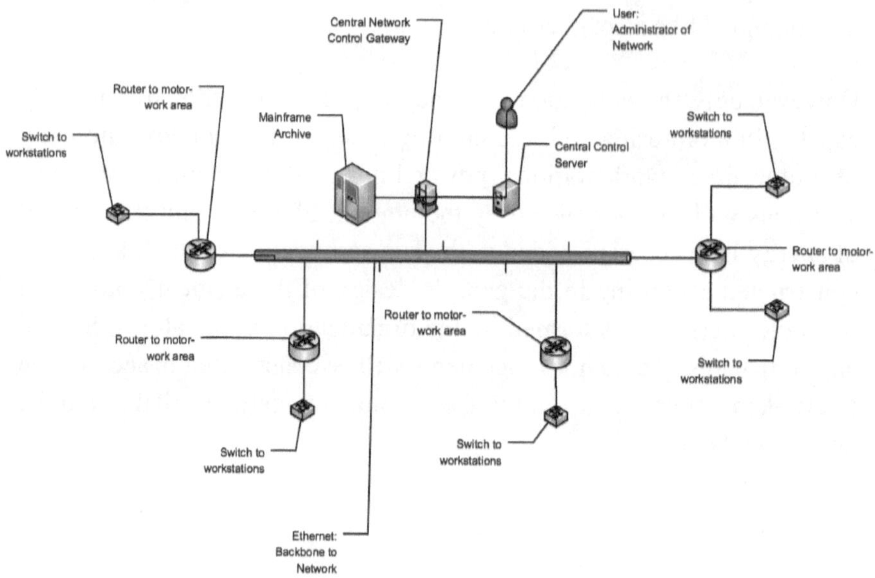

Fig 2[8],[9]

No matter how well built and how well programmed the central network
control is, the efficiency can only be as reliable as the user/administrator/
mind of the central processing system is. The user/administrator/mind
will make the final programming instructions to be given to the motor
areas and the work stations. The more complex the autonomous body is,
with a complex matrix of stations and motor areas, the longer it will take
to process all data coming into the central network control. It will take
long to process the incoming data, evaluate the processed data, and then

---

[8] The network matrix of stations, work areas, and central network control has been
constructed by the Visio 2007 program.

User is linked to the Central Control Server to relate to the cybernetic network
system and communicate with the net;

The Central Control Gateway is connected to the Mainframe archive that holds
long term memories of programs and files,

The Central Control Gateway is connected to the Ethernet backbone to for strong
link to the all 'Router to motor areas' of the network;

Each Router is connected to a switch to workstations.

[9] The power line is separate from the communication line (the cybernetic network
system); but travels along the same pathway.

send the response through the matrix to the specific stations and areas to manipulate and maneuver the autonomous body.

The motor in the central network control will have much work to do. This area will need much refined fuel for energy and matter to operate and fulfill its duty. All stations and areas in the complex autonomous body will have to do their share of work to provide the residually refined fuel (amplified energy impulses) and circulate the fuel to the central network control's motor.

The more work the central network control has to do in processing and controlling the work stations and motor areas, the more energy and matter it will require. The more work the processor has to do, the less work space and memory space it will have to hold incoming data to be processed and worked on. Response will be slow. If the stations and motor areas are not prepared or trained to deal with the situation(s), the central network control will have to do much work to process incoming data, be programmed for new instructions and then control the station(s) and area(s) directly to react. Station(s) and area(s) may have difficulty(s) in gathering data and responding to it, but with time the central network control will, and administrator, have constructed enough programming to confront the situation automatically or have the station(s) and area(s) confront the situation automatically. Each station and each motor area will have been trained to react to the simulated situations and perform out of reflexive response without having to wait for the central network control to give any instruction.

EFFECTS BY THE JOINT EFFORT

Effect of body on the surrounding environment

An autonomous structure consists of many mechanisms that maintains it and enables it to be self sufficient with the resources provided to it from the surrounding environment. The generic design of the object begins at the sub-atomic structure and design of the atoms of the elements used in constructing the mass autonomous structure. The sub-atomic nodes recognized in quantum will determine the design of the atom and how it will relate with other elements. The elements joined together will form molecules. These molecules will be tempered and organized to build mechanisms and devices.

Along with mechanisms that are built for use, the elements and molecules will also be used to form energy and matter to be used to maintain, operate, and possibly refine the construction of the devices.

An android is a sophisticated machinery that simulates the physiology of the human body, and motor body. The sophistication is the extreme amount of motor areas present in this machine's body to enable it to imitate the mobility and performance of the human body. To maintain, operate, and possibly refine the motor areas stations in the android's body, power source and mass of matter must be provided. A power source, fuel, will be created by the body from the resources and elements in the surrounding environment. This power (energy source and matter) will circulate around the body and amongst the motor areas and stations to provide what is needed.

All stations and motor areas must be in operation and functioning, at low level or high level, at all times. All stations and areas must be working in coordination with each other to provide the properly tempered fuel (tempered power source) and matter source that they will need from each other. There must be a plan of operation for all the stations and areas to operate in accordance with each other. All stations and areas in the power line must be fully functional to keep the energy source and mass of matter flowing through them. If there is no plan of operation and a purpose for the entire autonomous body, the energy and matter will be wasted away. The circulation of the energy source and matter will slow down or stop flowing. The entire autonomous body will become exhausted. It will take forever to reactivate the entire operational system of the power network and the motor areas in the autonomous body. The physical body of the autonomous body may be restored to its full operational capacity; but the managing operational system in the central network control may have to be reprogrammed again.

Control of the body by processing the communication network

By universal physics and mechanics, every motor area in the autonomous body will act and react predictably according to factors the area is faced with. The factors are its internal elements, the elements in the surrounding environment, and the physical force(s) the area will encounter. Every area has learned how to act and react according to the factors since the construction. With time, the area will face situations that will experience situations and factors that will require new ways of reacting and responding. The area will have to be given detailed instructions. Messages of actions will have to be sent through the communication line.

Control of the network by the central network

Data will be gathered at each motor area and its work stations. The motor area will react as it was trained to. To work in coordination with the areas, it was not given and received detailed messages, but instructions by physical impulses through the power lines. The power level and the amount of matter source that pass through the motor area will affect the impulse in the circulation. This reflexive reaction is mechanical (action leading to predictable reaction and predictable result).

If the central network control wishes to give any detailed instructions for the autonomous body to act beyond regular reflex, instruction and message will be sent through the communication line. The central network control does not have to give detail instructions to every motor area for specific action. The central control just sends detailed instruction(s) to specific area(s) to do something. As the area(s) perform as instructed, impulse will be triggered causing other area(s) to react mechanically.

The motor areas and work stations will send data to the central network control about what information they are receiving and what they are doing. If it is beyond the areas' and the stations' preprogramming, the CNC will process and determine if it has the preprogrammed memory to handle the situation. The central network control, the central processing center, will process the information and decide if it has information on how to deal with something like that. If the central network control has preprogrammed memory to deal with the situation, it will give automated instruction. If the situation is beyond the preprogrammed memory, the processed data will be sent to the administrator/user and mind to decide what new instruction will be given. The CNC, the central network control, will direct the station, the area, and the body into place to cause an impulse. Physics and mechanics will do the rest.

The droid and the automaton will perform as preprogrammed to. The droid is less intelligent then the automaton so it cannot perform sophisticated tasks requiring much program operations. A droid has no central network control to monitor a network of operations by a network of stations and areas. The android is like an automaton; like an automaton, it has a robotic body that can do sophisticated operation. An automaton has a central network control that will monitor a network of stations to operate in coordination with each other to enable complex operation by the robotic body of the automaton. Unlike an automaton, and android has such intelligence and preprogramming to construct new simple programs relating to the preprogrammed instructions and present data and situation.

> *Direct the body to the right place at the right time by momentum; then let physics and mechanics, working with Mother Nature and Father Time, do the rest.*

MECHANICAL DEFICIENCY

Deficient Resources

Raw resources from the surrounding environment provide the means for power, energy source and matter, required by the stations, the areas, and the autonomous body. The raw resources will be taken in to be refined to produce the energy source, along with the matter, to be used by the body and its parts. The produced fuel and power will provide the energy to do work, and the materials for the stations and areas to develop. As the body evolves, the stations and areas will evolve. The usage of the power levels will change. The facilities using the power and doing the work will have to change. These stations and areas will change to enhance the power to new power levels.

As the raw resources diminish, the amount of matter and energy level diminishes. The stations and areas will have little to nothing to build on. When one station or one area slows down or stops, the following stations and areas in the path of the power line will begin to slow down or stop. The primary control of the autonomous body, the central network control, will cease to function. The primary motor that operates the primary control will have lack of power, energy and matter resources, to operate.

Stage 1:   ***Sudden surprise to the autonomous body and structure has caused moment of disruption in regular routine.***

Deficiency in Power Production and Distribution

The efficiency in the operation of the stations, the areas and the autonomous body is only as good as the supply of energy and sources of matter that flow in the power line. The primary generator refines the raw materials from the external environment. The type of power source (supply of power) produced will determine how strong the amount of energy will be provided to do the necessary work by the station and area, and how rich the matter provided by this power will be.

Whether the power and fuel is rich or poor, that will depend on how well the generator that refines the raw resources is doing its work. It can produce rich fuel for the stations and areas to use and develop on. The stations and areas will develop rich and the enhanced power supply that will become very productive for the other stations and areas, and the body. If the power supply is poorly produced, the supply of power, level of energy source and matter may not have the sufficient capability to assist the damaged areas and stations to restore themselves. The matrix of stations and areas connected to this poorly supplied power line can and will eventually bring down the autonomous body. To save this damaged autonomous body, external assistance will be needed to repair the bad generator, enrich the bad power supply, and repair the damaged/damaging stations and areas.

Trading (distribution) of the power source is an impulse that enables work to be done. Trading is power providing energy to do work.

Stage 2:   ***Trading of resources is power; distribution of resources is power. Power in the network has been suspended:***

Deficiency in Communication Network Processing

The best way to maintain and operate a complex autonomous body would be by communication. This body will consist of a complex matrix of stations and motor areas to perform detailed motor operations by the body. The matrix of stations and areas will be linked with a power line. Communication amongst the stations and areas, and with the central network control, will be done by direct lining. A line, separate to the power line, will be constructed to link all stations and areas together and enable direct online communication.

If for any reason an area is damaged severing the communication, control of the area will be severed. The stations and areas will have to operate on their own (they are left on their own). The communication is intended to instruct the stations and areas on how to operate and use the power and matter source provided to them. If there is a power build up from the flow of power supply and there is no instruction or guidance on how to operate and use the power, the motor area will operate, by reflexive reaction, chaotically. This area of the body will go into 'convulsion'. This area is doing work with the fuel, power and energy present, but without guidance.

If something has happened causing the stations to have difficulty to relay the communication packets, the communication will be severed even if the power line has not. The matrix has gone into seizure now. Ability to communicate amongst the stations, and with the central network control, has been taken away or seized.

The most complex part of the communication network is in the central network control. If the communication linkage amongst the memory processing towers is in 'seizure', the entire matrix of the autonomous body will be in chaos. When the central network control is in chaos, there is no proper control and guidance of the rest of the body. All areas must be trained and prepared for suspensions, loss of connection with central control. The areas will have to work with each other by impulse through the power line. There will be no detail instructions; only reflexive reaction by physics and mechanics.

Stage 3:   ***Effort to maintain and control order through communication has been suspended:***

MATRIX OF THE VESSEL

An object lies on a table waiting to be dissected carefully. Before we enter it, we begin recording what has been taken noticed on the surface. The body has five areas extended outside of the body with connections to the body.

There is one external part that is different from the other four external parts. It is curved and rounded simulating an oval object with a bridge connecting to the rest of the body. It has six holes. Two holes are on opposite sides (opposite surfaces) of this oval object. There are two holes on the same surface; they are on the same parallel line and far away from the bridge. There are two small holes sharing the same parallel line and are closer to each other. This parallel line is closer to the bridge. There is a final hole that is even closer to the bridge.

There are two long objects that are on opposite sides on this long body. These long objects are on the upper area of this body near the bridge to the extended oval area. They are long with bent joining points simulating limbs. There are another two long objects that are on opposite sides of the body, just right under the upper extended areas on the same side as them. They simulate the upper limbs but longer. It is taken notice that the many joints on the limb enable each limb to do sophisticated operations outside of the body. This object with extended limbs enabling it motion and activities gives the impression that this object is a machine.

As we dissect into the body, there are many small objects simulating machines that are connected to each other. There is one set of lines that are connected to each small machine. The energy source and mass of matter are delivered through these areas will be identified as power lines. The machinery is designed and constructed for its specific purpose and function in the area it is located at. The energy and force provided by the amount of material traveling through these lines enables the momentum of the machine. The design of the machine will affect its motion affecting the momentum of material to the next machine. This is the effect of reflexive momentum. The reflexive momentum is recognized as a direct communication controlled by path of material flow (flow of energy pattern and level & pattern of force).

There are internal machineries for respiration; processing raw resources gathered externally; circulation of the newly produced power source and material source; internal and external momentum; and sensory(s). All machineries will be working coherently with each other. There is communication through the power line here is by reflexive response. There is no direct communication but response to momentum.

Should anything disrupt the flow of the material causing a build up with no or low level of free flow, the jointed area and its machineries will act erratically; convulsion will occur. There is free flow of material, energy and force; but there is limited amount of matter, the machinery(s) will react slowly or not at all. Because there is poor level of reflexive reaction by the small machineries in the large machinery body, the large machinery body becomes slow.

The masses of matter and energy source must be processed and developed into a form that the matrix of small machineries can use. A set of machineries will process the raw resources that will be gathered by the large autonomous body that holds the matrix of its smaller internal machineries. The small processing machineries will need processed and produced masses of matter and energy to operate by. These machineries will process a new supply of processed energy and matter for its matrix of small machineries to use. The internal machineries and large machinery will require oxygen or other usable gases to cool the machineries and its energy and matter masses when they are being worked upon and being delivered. The solid raw resources, liquid raw resources and gaseous raw resources will be needed to produce the type of refined energy and matter masses that will be used by the large machinery and its internal machineries.

The large autonomous body must gather the proper amount or raw resources to be processed to produce the energy and matter to be used by the matrix of internal machineries. The set of processing machineries must produce rich sources of energy and matter for the machineries to use productively. If the processing machineries produce rich sources, the matrix of machineries will perform richly and productively; the massive autonomous body will also perform richly and productively. If the processing machineries do not produce rich sources that will be used by the matrix of machineries, the machineries will not perform effectively and there may not be enough produced materials (matter) and energy for free flow through the power line. This can be disruptive to the reflexive reaction that controls the matrix of machineries.

This autonomous body is immobile and is being dissected for observation. It is immobile, but its internal mechanisms are still functioning; slow, some suspended, but still functional. Testing its coherency, joints are tapped expecting reaction. The area tapped is not the only location that is showing immediate reflexive reaction. Other areas linked to that joint are also responding. The free flow of power and material passing through the tapped area stimulates other areas to enable coordinated motion.

A jointed area on the upper left limb far from the body has been tapped. The tapping is light so only the smaller joints routed to the tapping area responds. It is not only the surface of the limb that is moving, but the internal machineries in this limb are also operating coherently. Energy source and matter free flowing through matrix on this limb build up at areas that are responding in motion. Areas that are not responding will let the sources flow freely through them. The machineries in the matrix will share the energy source and matter by not using when it is not needed and allowing others to use the sources when needed. This reflexive reaction will require free flow of power (energy source and matter). If there is no free flow, there will be a buildup of sources. This autonomous machinery and its matrix of sub-machineries will react erratically, convulse. Mechanical order and control in the reflexive response will have been seized or taken away (seizure).

Along with a set of power lines connected through this matrix of machineries, there is also a set of power lines that deliver only impulses of electricity, not energy source and matter. Each machinery is designed to receive specific signals for specific actions. This intranet of electrical signals is maintained by a central network control that processes the electrical signals; the CNC controls the traffic of network signals. This processor will instruct the matrix network of machineries as it was preprogrammed and trained to. It will receive further instructions externally to guide the internal machineries to perform coherently for specific purposes. The central network control will guide the matrix of machineries until the matrix have been reformulated to perform reflexively. If the machineries can perform reflexively, the central network control will not have to spend time guiding the matrix of machineries and continue monitoring the external performance of the mass autonomous body. If the intranet is ever severed at any point, there will be no guidance to the matrix. The CNC will not process and give instructions. It will no longer give traffic messages as automatically as preprogrammed to. If the internal machineries and the autonomous machinery encounter a situation they are not preprogrammed to, they will perform erratically. Orderly control by the central network control will have been seized or taken away (seizure). If sudden situations causing disruption in the central network processing system keep occurring, it will take time to notice a pattern of the occurrences to formulate a reflexive response toward the difficulty.

An android's anatomic structure simulates the anatomic structure of a human body, or an animal body. It's an automaton (a sophisticated robot) that can do any motor operation the human can. An android has a very large and intelligent central network control. It can be preprogrammed to have the CNC produce programs on its own as programmed to. The present space ship simulates the capabilities of a robot but does not have the features of an android or an automaton that is simulating an animal or a humanoid. The hull simulates the body of an animal swimming in the water. The large aft thrusts at the stern (rear of the ship) simulate the legs of the body directing the body to go forward. The impulse holes at the bow of the ship (the front of the ship) and the stern of the ship directs the ship to go upward or downward from its present position (the pitch). The impulse holes to the port side (the left side) and the starboard side (the right side) of the ship will direct the ship to go left or right from its present position (the yaw). The impulse holes on the upper side and lower side of the port and the starboard sides will determine the roll of the ship from its present position.

The Bernoulli's Principle concentrates on how pressure force on the mass will direct the pathway and position of the mass. There is no counter force in motion in the vacuum of space. The impulse holes will provide pressure forces that will determine the pathway and position of the space ship. The pressure force from the impulse holes on the upper side and lower side on the starboard side and port side will determine the roll of the ship. The upper holes on the star board side and the lower holes on the port side will have the ship rolling toward the star board side. The Holes of the lower side of the bow will have the ship pitching upward.

In the vacuum of space, anything in motion with an applied force will stay in motion at the same speed and applied force. To stop the ship from motion, the aft thrust will stop and all impulse holes will direct pressure force forward. The impulse holes will continue until the ship stops moving.

The UFS Jonathan is locked in the 'dry dock' at a port in the Alpha Space Station. The Jonathan is fully powered and operational. The botanical garden (farm) is in full function with all food supplements planted. All provisions are stored. All living areas and resting lounges are ready for usage. All stations and departments all around the ship are manned and fully operational. All are waiting order from the bridge to direct the Jonathan out of the 'dry dock' and move onward to the outer orbit by impulse before leaving the solar system by hyper space.

The CNC of UFS Jonathan, identified as Jonathan, works subconsciously with intelligence with the senior officers and the crew on board. Jonathan has subconscious intelligence, but it has no sentient life (no self-awareness). The captain and the senior officers are the self-aware life of Jonathan.

The 1st Engine is active but not at full power. Captain Jameson instructs the helm officer to activate Jonathan to full power. The helms officer directs message through the ionic gas to the engine room to activate the 1st Engine to full power providing full power to the entire vessel. The Captain then instructs the helm officer to disengage from clamps of the 'dry dock'. Once the clamps are released, the helms officer instructs Jonathan to get out of the 'dry dock'. There is no unpredictable motion and activity so the CNC directs the impulse from the aft thrust to move the ship out of port. Since this motion is regular, every details of the motor operation operate by programmed calculations.

The Jonathan moves toward the outer orbit position by impulse power. When the Jonathan reaches its position in the outer orbit of the solar system, the helms officer enters the calculated program onto the Jonathan to navigate to the far destination by bent space and time (quantum tunnel and hyper-space) created by the hyper drive engine. After receiving programmed instruction, the CNC of the Jonathan goes toward the destination automatically. If there is nothing irregular in the activity(s) and operation of the Jonathan, the crew will do their routine of research and logging of their works.

The CNC in the Jonathan will carry out the procedures and maneuvers of the vessel as it was programmed to. The programmed procedures and maneuvers are formulated in response to the variables of time, space and matter. If the formulations and the variables do not coordinate, the CNC will construct a new formulation in accordance with what it already knows and how to relate with the present variables; by the judgment of the seniors and the crew.

Each manned station can be recognized as a cellular station the way each molecular-cellular pack in the power line and in the communication line is. Each cellular station will require power to operate. At full power, each area will be provided with a store of energy so each station will be provided as much power the station will need to operate at full capacity. All stations will have definite somatic capability. For proper and accurate mobility and detection, the vessel must be able to touch and feel inside and outside of itself at each area. The CNC will work with each station at each area to respond to what has been detected at the station and area. Whatever has happened, the CNC will report what has happened to the seniors at the bridge, and the crewmember(s) at the local station and area. If the situation is orthodox, the CNC will react automatically. If the situation is unorthodox, the crewmember(s) will report what is happening to the bridge for command. If the situation cannot wait for response from the bridge, the crewmember will act by his own self-awareness and give his command to the station and the CNC; he will take responsibility for his immediate action.

As the Jonathan travels through its hyperspace, each station will report what is happening and how the crew and the vessel is responding to the conditions. This is a research vessel and this is the first time a ship is traveling great distance through hyperspace. Every moment must be recorded in detail. The CNC is preprogrammed to take notice of the audio, visual, gustatory, olfactory and somatic experiences and report every detail. Action will be left to the officers on the bridge and to the crewmember(s) at the local station(s) and area(s).

After a brief moment in the long distance hyper-drive tunnel, the Jonathan comes out far from the home solar system. This region, Quadrant A, is unknown to Earth. The science crew must now begin mapping the stars and planets of this Quadrant A. The Jonathan must now travel at impulse power from aft thrust, with mobile guidance from the impulse holes all around the vessel. The Jonathan will be protected in its own hyperspace dimension.

Coming out of the womb, the protected environment known as United Federation, UFS Jonathan must learn how to use its features outside of protected space. While the Jonathan is traveling through the region Quadrant A, she moves at impulse researching the surroundings. All stations and areas expect to receive full power to operate accurately. Engineering Room has reported that the 1st Engine and 2nd Engine are running at full capacity and are producing power at full level. Once entering Quadrant A, CNC and the stations are reporting to the bridge that they are receiving low level of power.

Lt. Cmd. Mat tells Cpt. Jameson:

> "The Engineering Room is fine but we are not running at full power. There may be disruption in the power line somewhere. There is power provided for regular operations. Excess power for operations beyond regular routine (repairs and adjustments) is not present. There is leakage of power due to damage in the power line, but the local station(s) cannot locate and repair the damage."

Capt. Jameson responds with:

> "Full stop, slow down all operation; shut down all non-essential operation. Suspend the operations but do not shut down the stations. Find the problem Mat."

Cmd. Mat looks through the schematics of Jonathan's power line set up with the CNC. The CNC reports that there is a light damage at the 1st Lounge; the damage is not severe and the station, the area, should have been able to repair itself automatically. Cmd. Mat goes to the lounge and looks at the damage and the power line. He agrees with the CNC that the station and area should have been able to repair the light damage. He then looks at the power line. He notices that the power line is damaged but not severe. He then looks into the power line at the power packs. He notices that the power level is not as rich (as active) as expected.

At the meeting of the senior officers, Capt. Jameson tells all that there is power loss. Lt. Cmd. Mat reports that the engines are running finely, and the damage in the 1st Lounge was not severe and should had been able to repair itself with the level of power that is expected in the power line. He then states that the energy source in the molecular-cellular packs is not at full capacity. He suggests that there may be defect in the 1st Engine or the 2nd Engine; the 1st Engine is not producing the type of power expected, or the 2nd Engine is not producing the correct molecular-cellular packs needed to carry proper power level required by the vessel.

Capt. Jameson concludes with:

> "UFS Jonathan is fine so the mission will carry on without any difficulty. The only problem we have is either power production or power distribution. The problem is not severe; if something occurs to the vessel it will take longer than usual to repair the damage. We must avoid all situations that can cause damage to the vessel, if possible. If something does happen, we must get to safety to do whatever repair possible before we confront the situation (manually). While we wait, we must use our time productively and research what had happened and learn from it. The UFS Jonathan is a prototype vessel. We can expect problems with power production, power distribution, damage occurrences, etc. We just report it, study it, and continue on with our mission without disturbance."

The power line passes through each station and each area delivering power. The power must be kept circulating. All stations will be kept active, at full capacity or not. All areas will receive the necessary amount of power to maintain its operation to serve the ship (the vessel and crew). When new area(s) and new station(s) are built as the ship evolves, a new pathway(s) through the station(s) will be constructed to direct the amount of power and store of energy for all station(s) and area(s) to operate coherently.

Should power build up because an area is not using the power and store of energy being delivered there, this store of power will create its own action causing incoherent reflexive reaction amongst the area(s). This action is happening without control. Control has been seized; seizure due to uncontrolled reflexive reaction.

The Jonathan has just encountered a wave of force when it entered into Quadrant A and stopped. This force affected an area on the vessel causing a stoppage in the area. This area and several other areas will act incoherently with the rest of the network. The CNC reports this to the Engineer on the bridge.

Cmd. Mat tells Capt. Jameson:

"Several areas on the vessel are acting incoherently."

Capt. Jameson responds with:

"All stop. Go check on the problem."

Lt. Cmd. Mat asks the CNC:

"What started the incoherency?"

The CNC responds with:

"A station in storage area A is damaged during the counter wave. The damaged station caused its area to shut down. Other areas linked to this area's actions responded resulting in incoherency toward the rest of the vessel."

Cmd. Mat reactivates the damaged station and area. The other areas responded with coherency to the rest of the vessel. The Engineering returns to the Capt. Jameson telling him that the problem has been handled.

Lt. Cmd. Mat informs Capt. Jameson with:

> "Should area(s) be shut down incoherently, the rest of the vessel will respond and operate incoherently. The vessel will be out of control until repairs are made."

Lt. Cmd. Mat informs the seniors:

> "If a charge of energy and power affects an area and station causing a discrepancy, the path of the power line will be disrupted causing incoherency in the reflexive reaction; other areas will not be performing as they are expected to. Seizing control of reflexive reaction will occur."

Power must be kept flowing. There will be no hoarding. If there is a buildup of power in any area leading to no free flow, the vessel will eventually go into chaos; the ship (vessel and crew) will go into chaos.

NETWORK GUIDANCE

An automaton consists of many mechanisms. The many mechanisms working together coherently enable the automaton to operate automatically. To enable coherency, all mechanisms in the autonomous body are joined together in a communication network. A communication line connecting the mechanisms together enables the mechanisms to communicate with each other and enable all to work together by knowing what is needed.

The Jonathan has a mass communication network that holds the matrix of mechanisms together. The mechanisms are stations and work areas (lounges, rooms, gardens, labs, etc.). The communication line consists of ionized gas that produces and delivers energy packets. Each packet consists of the address from the sender, the address to the recipient, the travel route to the recipient, the security condition, and the detailed message. Each station has been preprogrammed to read specific messages and respond accordingly to the message received. The station has been preprogrammed during construction on how it shall operate in that work area. The crew man working at the station will work with the CNC and the officers at the bridge to develop new procedures and maneuvers for the station's operational system to remember and know. Drills will be held consistently to develop the procedures and maneuvers. The communication line will enable the stations of the area to work with each other and improve the operation of the area. The communication of the areas will improve the operation of the vessel.

Each station will have a definite capacity to detect somatically, and direct the crew man and the drones of the station to respond somatically. Since the internal environment on the Jonathan is gaseous to support the crew and gardens, the internal stations and internal areas will have capacity to detect by audio, visual, gustatory, olfactory along with somatic sensory. The vacuum has no need of smelling or tasting, the outer hulls will only activate audio, visual and somatic sensory all around the outer hull. Even when the Jonathan is in its hyperspace (hyperspace at all times), the sensors will still be able to detect outside of the hyper space barrier.

The Jonathan, crew and vessel, was preprogrammed and trained for expected occurrences; preparations and trainings were done in confined and protected environments. There was no true understanding of what to expect in real space or how to deal with it. When the big wave brought mass turbulence onto the Jonathan, the power network, the communication network, all station areas, and the crew were in shock. In a confined testing area, all areas of the vessel will work with each other and set out proper amounts of force through their impulse holdings like a vessel under water. The vessel intends to maintain buoyancy as it encounters turbulence force or as it moves. In an automated vessel, all areas will have been trained and prepared to deliver force coherently without waiting for central control. They will be acting by reflexive reaction even without direct communication.

The bridge is the brain in the Jonathan. The senior officers, and bridge officers, at their consoles are the lobes in the brain (audio, visual, gustatory, olfactory, and somatic. The CNC (Central Network Control) is the CNS and brain stem directing the traffic of the communication made through the network of ionized gas lines. To maintain coherency, each area will report what is happening, how it acts and what assistance it will expect from the rest of the vessel. The CNC is the central archive on planned strategy; it will give instruction to the entire vessel on what plan is to be taken and all areas will act as trained to in accordance to the specific plan. After the CNC gives instruction on the plan to be taken, all areas of the vessel will be on their own. Every area will work accordingly and on schedule. If there was never a proper plan for a specific situation, the entire ship will be in chaos waiting for the incident to happen and in chaos as it tries to recover from the incident.

As the Jonathan came out of the hyper-drive tunnel, a meteor was passing by. It was large and fast. As the large meteor was rushing across the Jonathan's path, it was pushing a great wave of force. The Jonathan was rolling around out of control in space like a submarine would be rolling out of control in deep water once a big turbulence force has pushed on it.

The 1st wave as the meteor pushes is strong. A moment after the 1st Wave, the tail will bring the 2nd Wave. The 2nd Wave will not be as strong as the 1st, but it will bring to whatever is in the meteor's path.

After the 1st Wave, the Jonathan was rolling out of control. The 1st Lounge was off line as the CNC reported. The 1st Lounge was not the only area in trouble. All stations and areas reported to the bridge that the communication lines were out and the power lines were out. The gravitational field was fine. The crews reported of shock and did not know what was happening and what to expect.

Cmd. Carl reported:

> "There are crews with broken arms, but all did report of great fear and anxiety, There is no severe damage, but a brief medical leave for everybody can be helpful to relieve their stress."

Lt. Cmd. James reported:

> "Communication network is down. The communication line has been severed at several areas due to the mass force due to the lack of preparation from the mass coming force. The stem from the bridge to the rest of the vessel stations is in chaos. There was no substitute plan to compensate for any sudden situation like this. It will take a while to repair the damaged communication lines. We need to work with the CNC to make repairs and preparation for pending situations."

Lt. Cmd. Mat reported:

> "The frame structure of the vessel is fine, but areas of the vessel are in disruption. Station consoles have fallen out of place. Power lines have been severed due to the massive force. There was no substitute plan in preparation for this so everything is still in chaos. There will be temporary repairs on the severed areas of the severed power line, but

will take a while to make full repairs. We will need the CNC to work with us to repair and maintain the power lines."

Lt. Cmd. Kevin reported:

"The first time man has ever seen a meteor passing this close. We should have prepared our sensors to detect anything that suddenly happens and detect life (sentient or physical) and element contents of what passes by. Man has seen meteors come and go but we have never studied what are on them. We must reprogram the vessel to automatically gather data of what excitement occurs and do immediate research without having to wait for the bridge to give the command through the CNC."

Lt. Cmd. Xiao reported:

"The crew all over the vessel were exited and scared. There was sudden noises but there were no violence. There was a moment of disorientation but people went back to their posts."

Lt. Mans reported:

"The situation with the crew is just as Cmd. Xiao has reported. The containers did fall out place all over the vessel. Station Consoles did fall out of place due to the massive turbulence leaving the person(s) in charge of the station confused with what to do. We need a plan for everybody to continue on with their work whenever something does occur causing a temporary disruption in the routines. This can prevent chaos. Work will continue and enable all stations to assist when needed."

Under the advice of the seniors, a plan will be constructed. Captain Jameson stated that the Jonathan will have to construct a plan by trial and error.

Captain Jameson stated:

> "It is understood that plan(s) will be constructed for specific circumstances. We will have to determine how to identify what the pending situation may be. We will have to determine what kind of plan will be best in dealing with the situation. We will prepare ourselves by trial and error. There will be drills to prepare all to operate at their stations, and to operate at the facility area."

> "There must be communication amongst the areas. The bridge will monitor that traffic of the communication of the areas."

The communication system/network is the basis in control and order in the ship (crew and vessel). In the conference of the seniors, Lt. Cmd. James gave a brief explanation of how the communication network works and how it affects the ship. He explained how the communication network is setup. The communication network is a matrix of work stations (communication outlets).

Lt. Cmd. James:

> "Each station is a cell in the matrix of the communication network. Each station has been previously programmed, and is continuously being reprogrammed, for specific operation(s). Each station has specific duty(s) that program(s) will enable the station(s) to do. The program(s) will enable the station to operate automatically by sub-conscious intelligence. The crew member(s) manning the station will be the self-awareness of the station. The self-awareness at the station will enable the station to operate with conscious intelligence."

Lt. Cmd. James points to the monitor and the devices in the conference room and continues with:

> "The CNC manages and controls the entire operation and traffic of the network. The CNC is not the network, but the center of the communication network in the Jonathan. The entire network of stations, with the vessel and the crew, is the ship UFS Jonathan. The entire communication is a system of communication that maintains the operation of the UFS Jonathan."

Lt. Cmd. James then points to the seniors, and to him, and continues with:

> "The entire network simulates a massive computer entity. Each computer has a processor; the larger the computer, the larger the processor and a large hard drive archive. The CNC is the mass processor that manages the entire network. The seniors on the bridge are the self-aware consciousness user of the communication network of UFS Jonathan, the UFS Jonathan."

> "The CNC is the mass processor of the mass computer, the mass computer network on the Jonathan. The station at each point on the network (mass computer) is a sub-processor. It needs only a sufficient amount of power to do its work there. Combined together, entire network and ship will use a large amount of power. The CNC and the bridge will need a large amount of power, and possibly more, to monitor and control the entire network and ship. The bridge and the CNC use the most power on the ship."

> "The CNC and its hard drive are the mass processor and archive in the massive network and massive computer called the communication network. The RAM (Random Access Memory) of this large computer consists of many sub-processors called stations at each point in the network, at each point in the vessel. The HD archive at each station

becomes a piece of the work memory of the massive RAM of the massive computer called the communication network of the ship (the vessel and crew). The CNC is the massive processor and archive of this massive computer. The user of this massive computer is the bridge (the seniors and officers on the bridge)."

He continues:

"The ship's walls and facilities will expand. To meet the requirements, the communication networks will expand having cables and wirings adjusted with the change of the hull and the means for the ship to confront the environments it will encounter. With the changes of the cables and the purpose of usages, the wirings, the stations and the entire network will be reprogrammed at every moment. This ship and its hull will evolve for other ships to learn and develop from."

Lt. Cmd. James was not theatrical when he presented his statement about the ship and its communication network.

FLIGHT PLANS

Captain Jameson and his crew took the UFS Jonathan out of the 'dry dock' in space the same way the captains and crews did with their other ships. It was done as trained and planned in the academy. All stations were at full operation but at low power waiting to respond at any moment response must be made. The primary engine is operating at full power to provide only impulse speed and much power for immediate response at each station if an immediate response must be made.

Captain Jameson gives the command:

"Disengage from the clamps."

Once the ship leaves port and is distant from the space station dock, the Captain instructs the helmsman to go to the outer orbit of the solar system at half impulse speed. The entire ship was pre-instructed on how their mission will begin, leaving the port and going straight out to the outer orbit before going to full quantum light speed (warp speed through a quantum tunnel formed by the hyper drive engine on board the UFS Jonathan).

As the UFS Jonathan reaches the outer orbit, all are ready for the effects of entering from a naturally created universal environment to a controlled quantum environment created. This is going to be the first time man will be travelling at the speed of light (light is no longer the c constant but a c variable). Since this the first time man has travelled with this kind of vessel and this kind of power, the UFS Jonathan will be writing a new manual on how to travel in space and how man will have to perform technically, mentally, physically, socially, diplomatically psychologically.

Once reaching Quadrant A, Capt. Jameson requests for all his seniors to meet with him at the conference room (the Ready Rm.). He discusses about plan(s) new to the General Plans from the Academy's trainings will be prepared from UFS Jonathan's maneuvers and operations from here on.

Capt. Jameson:

"Cmd. Johns, you are the Executive Officer; you are responsible with the administrative affairs of the crew and the internal operations of the entire ship. You will be assigning people to their duty areas and assignments according to their qualifications. Lt. Mans, you will report on the personal conditions of the staff and how they are at their posts and this voyage. We need to know how the ship will perform during unpredictable circumstances. You will work with Mr. Johns, head of administrations and internal operations."

Capt. Jameson continues:

"Man is about to involve himself in a new environment and atmosphere. The physical reaction of the human body toward these environments will be different. We will be entering into a controlled quantum matrix environment to travel at variable light speed. We will be travelling far and entering into planet space(s) with atmosphere different from what Man has been comfortable with through the ages. These planet space(s) will be inhabited by intelligent sentient beings with their own cultural practices. Though armed and manned by a military crew, this is a scientific and diplomatic vessel. We are to research and gather information on the physical condition of the regions. We are to gather information about the cultures and their social-psychological behaviors without bringing any disruption on their daily routines."

Capt. Jameson continues:

"This is going to be a long voyage. We will be far from the culture we have been accustomed to. This can affect the mentality of the crew. Dr. Carl and Dr. Simmons, you two will work together to study the crews physical conditions and their emotional and psychological conditions. Ms. Kevin, you will be gathering data and studying the environment and the life forms that are in the regions of space we will enter. Ms. Mat, you will be in consistent awareness of this vessel's engines and power systems. You will make consistent reports on how the engines are producing the power to produce the quantum matrix barrier for us to travel at variable light speed. We must know how long we can hold this matrix barrier and how far we can travel. You will be working with Ms. Kevin to gather new technology(s), power production and power sources."

"Ms. Xiao, you are the security officer. You are responsible for the internal security on board UFS Jonathan, and the defense of UFS Jonathan from external encounters (hostile or natural)."

"The UFS Jonathan is a new class of vessel with new ways of doing things. We will be writing a new manual on how all our ships and teams will operate. We must remember that the 'away team' that will be sent to go into the planetary space and confront the atmosphere directly must consist of at least one member from each department. Detailed reports must be made of every 'away' mission, of every encounter experienced and of every research done."

"Mr. Johns, you will work with Ms. Mans to prepare drills to train the crew to develop their routine capabilities. They must be able to get to their stations and perform better than expected. They must be able to consistently develop their performance and develop their stations' computer operations. This ship's crew will be divided into 3 shifts so they can get their necessary rest and be able to get to their stations fresh and strong to carry out their duties."

DISCREPANCIES IN THE OPERATION

The UFS Jonathan was constructed in the 'dry dock' of the Alpha Space Station. As the she left the Alpha Station and then the outer orbit of this solar system Earth is in, UFS Jonathan left the womb of United Federation. As the UFS Jonathan entered into Quadrant A of the galaxy, she stumbled like a toddler stumbles in his first attempt to walk.

Captain's Log: Capt. Jameson: 22200921   *(yyyymmdd)*:

"This is our first experience with massive wave turbulence. The ship had a gravitational field internally to hold its contents and passengers in position. All balanced along with the ship as she travelled. No matter how fast or slow, the ship and its gravitational field was prepared to the change in position. The sudden wave turbulence affected the ship without warning. The ship was not prepared for the change so all its contents were forced out of position. We will prepare ourselves for further surprises such as sudden turbulence. All areas will be prepared for sudden lock downs when sudden turbulence occurs."

"We are new to sudden turbulences. The hull of the vessel will require some adjustments. The Engineering Department will have to find means to make developments on the surface design and structural adjustments. They will work with the Science Department to understand what can be expected in space and the regions we will be traveling to. With the knowledge of the environments and the possible effects, Engineering will understand what adjustments may be needed."

"With the change in the hull and the areas, the Communication Department will work with Engineering to develop the new layouts for the communication cables and network. All stations and areas must work coherently with each other. When sudden turbulence occurs, the different areas and different stations must work together without the guidance of the CNC and the Bridge. The Communication Department must develop means to communicate with others outside of the ship. Communication Department will work with the Science Department to understand how the life forms communicate. Means to communicate with the other life forms will be established. The environment will affect the energy flow and the means to deliver the messages throughout the network in the ship. Communications, Engineering and Science will work together to improve energy flow and communication."

"The Jonathan is 'young' and still has much to learn. We will stay in Quadrant A and learn what this vessel and what this crew have. We must concentrate on developing the plan(s) for how the ship (the crew and its vessel) will develop and operate by."

The UFS Jonathan is new and the design of its hull and engine is new. She has just created a quantum barrier to pass through a hyper-tunnel it has also created. The power producing engine has created much power to be used at hyper speed. Lt. Cmd. Mat must now review the engine, the hull and the power network that delivers the power throughout the vessel. She must record everything she finds on to her log.

Engineer's Log: Cmd. Mat: 22200922:

"The 1st Engine worked out well as expected. The necessary amount of power to create the ship's barrier and the hyper tunnel for the ship to travel through was sufficient."

"When we came out of the tunnel, we encountered massive wave turbulence. The ship went on a roll. Because we were not prepared for the turbulence and the roll, damages occurred. Power was needed at regions on the ship to repair the damages to the hull. The power provided could power up the stations for regular operations; but when damaged, the stations could not operate effectively to repair and sustain the location. Was this due to fault in the station or fault in the power produced?"

"The hull has shown some damage. Severe damage leading to power leaks could not be repaired automatically through the stations in the locations as designed. Since the power delivered cannot power up the station(s) to do the necessary repairs, crew will have to do manual repairs with assistance from the stations, not vice versa as intended."

The strong wave turbulence caused damage to the communication system also. It is expectable that external reception by audio, gustatory, somatic and visual sensory was disrupted. The internal sensory were intended to sustain itself and repair all damages automatically. The sensory operated efficiently as Jonathan came out of the tunnel. After the turbulence, the sensory went and the internal communication network went into chaos. The CNC and the bridge were out of control.

Communication Officer's Log: Lt. Cmd. James: 22200922

"Internal communication and external communication were fine as we left outer orbit and entered into Quadrant A. Once we encountered mass turbulence, power and communication were out of order. The 2nd Engine may not be producing the energy packets efficiently. It may have been damaged. It appears that the poorly produced energy packets are delivering energy charges along with the messages. Disruption in any sensory can cause an unexpected charge in the communication network. The imbalanced charge will be sent to the CNC and primary processor. The CNC processor will be disrupted; the entire network and all areas will be disrupted."

"Whether the 2nd Engine/1st Engine is repaired or not, all areas must learn how to operate coherently without the guidance of the primary processor and the mass archive. There will be no primary intelligence. Everything will be done by work memory at each station. The areas will have to rely on reflexive reaction. The HD archive and the RAM at each station will have to become the work memory of the local station. The work memory and the operations of the local station must be kept active at every moment of the journey. If there is no primary instruction, each station will have to operate by the instruction/program that is left on the RAM."

Study of the environment is the responsibility of the Science Department.

Science Officer's Log   Lt. Cmd. Kevin: 22200922

"There was no general plan on how to gather information without disturbing the culture and environment. Any person from each Department will be part of an away team and get to an area in the region to gather information. People were startled in their first unexpected experience in deep space. There will be trainings for future unexpected experiences that will occur for the benefit of science."

There was disruption from regular routines.

Staff Officer's Log: Lt. Mans: 22200922

"The stations were operational during and after the turbulences. During the first turbulence, people were knocked out their posts, but they went back. After the second turbulence, people were frightened and walked off their stations, but went back. They weren't prepared for this."

"The gravitational field was out for a moment. Without gravitational field, objects floated out of place. New means of locking down objects at their places will have to be created."

"In the gardens, the loose soils floated out of place. In the labs, glasses floated out of place. Once gravitational field was regained, the soils fell down causing a mess in the gardens. The glass containers fell on the floors shattering all over. It was a mess in the labs."

BIO-ORGANIC AUTONOMY

BUILDING BLOCK OF THE HUMAN BODY

Conception / creation of the map and design of the human body

The technical term for the human species is Homo-Sapiens Erectus. This form of life on planet Earth is made of molecular compounds that consist of the element called Carbon. The Homo-Sapiens Erectus can also be recognized as a carbon based flesh-& blood life form. A carbon compound will mix with other compounds that will accept each other and work with each other. These carbon based compounds will have the capacity of organisms to respond to stimuli by reproduction and development. This body of molecular compounds that enables the body with the capacity of an organism makes the body a life form.

The building block of a large complex body of large carbon based life form begins as a minute carbon based organism called cell. There are different cells for different operations, and different purposes. The different cells are formed with different molecular compounds at different levels of energy. The different levels of energy will enable the carbon based compound to react and join with different elemental compounds and perform differently.

Carbon based compounds:

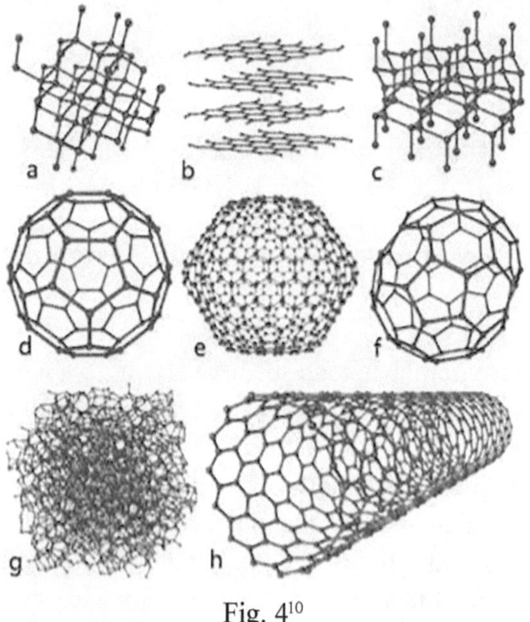

Fig. 4[10]

Cellular molecule

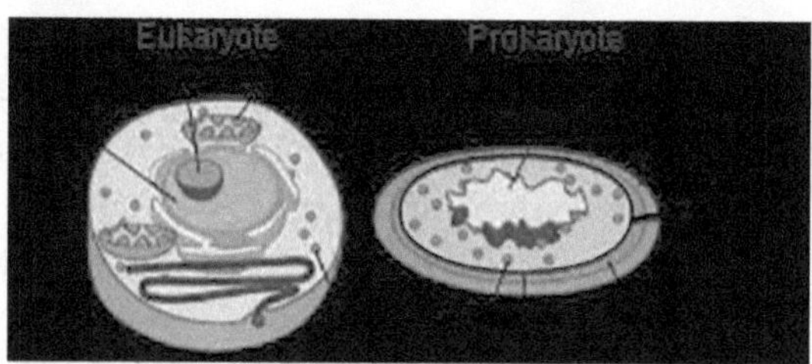

Fig. 5[11]

The sub-atom is the generic design of the atom. Energy and generic design of the element determines the generic design of the molecular compound, the cell. The generic design of the cell, genetics, is the generic design for the motor areas within the body. The generic design of the cellular compound with the elemental compounds in the environment will affect the construction of the body.

---

[10] Wikipedia, "Carbon", http://en.wikipedia.org/wiki/Carbon.

[11] Wikipedia, "Cell (Biology)", http://en.wikipedia.org/wiki/Cell_%28biology%29.

Each cell is a work station. Work stations combined will form the motor area. Cellular organisms (work stations) will form the sub-body motor organism (motor area). Cellular organisms in the blood will provide power, energy to do work, by impulse. Momentum by the blood flow forms the momentum to enable the organism to evolve and do work. As the organism evolves, it triggers the momentum and impulse in the blood flow.

Construction of the body and the blood vessels

Raw resource from the environment, food and nutrition, will be consumed into the autonomous body through the 'mouth' and refined by the generating sector call the 'digestive system'. The refined fuel and power source (nutrients) are produced from nourishment/food to be carried in cells. The cells travel through the power line called blood vessels. The nutrients in cells in the blood vessels are called plasma/blood. They carry the energy source and masses of matter to the joints and motor areas to reproduce, develop and operate. The body consists of the same type of plasma throughout the body, but at different compound level for different purposes. The design of the blood vessel will be according the generic design of the cell and operation of the motor area. Impulses of the blood will direct instructions from area to area for reflexive coordination.

While the body of the embryo and child is being developed, the mechanisms, motor areas and power lines (blood vessels) are forming. Each area and mechanism is learning and training by experience with each other as the body develops. The amount of motor areas and the size of the mechanisms will expand enabling the body to perform with complexity. All organisms must be active to circulate the blood supply throughout the body. The richer the blood supply, the more work the organisms can do. The poorer the blood supply, the lesser the work done by the organisms.

Blood Vessels

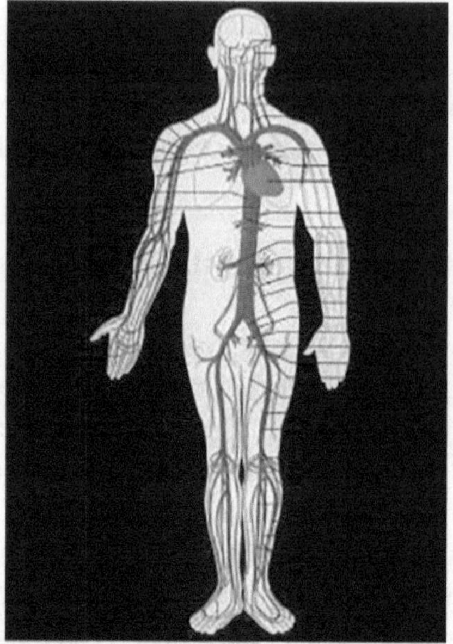

Fig. 6[12]

Creation of the communication network

Detailed messages and instructions will be delivered through a matrix of communication networks call nerves. The cells in the nerves are called neurons. They transmit packets of energy that hold pieces of the message. The neuron cell simulates a work station in a cybernetic network. Each station has the responsibility in receiving the packet(s) of the message, enhancing the energy level of the packet, and relaying the message onto the route to the direct recipient(s) of the message.

---

[12] Wikipedia, "Blood Vessel", http://en.wikipedia.org/wiki/Blood_vessel.

Nervous System (network of nerves in the body)

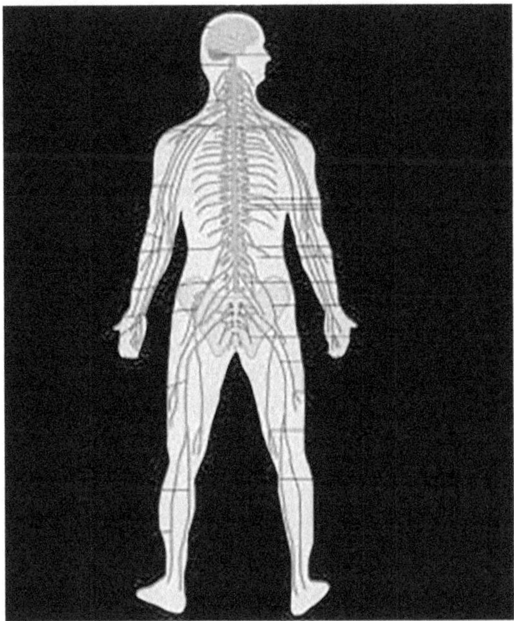

Fig. 7[13]

The neuron cell(s) will direct the motor area(s) to respond by releasing an electrical energy. The motor area(s) will respond to each other's impulses by reflexive action. Hormones and adrenaline masses will affect the blood flow affecting the reflexive response of the mechanism and the motor area(s). The neuron will direct the area into place. Physics and mechanics will do the rest.

---

[13] Wikipedia, "Nervous System", http://en.wikipedia.org/wiki/Neural_system.

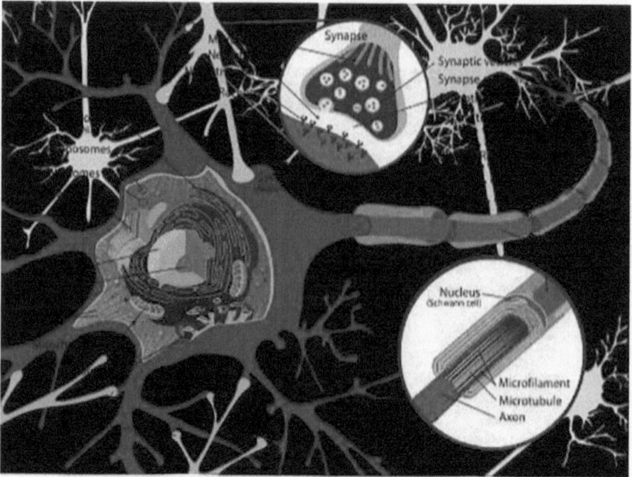

Fig. 8[14]

The generics/genetics of the molecules start with the sub-atom and the atom of the element. The genetic designs of the molecules form the map of the autonomous body, the animal body. It is the map of the body and its cells or organisms (the stations and motor areas of the autonomous body). It is not the map of the mind, the person. The power supply, the matter source in the cells, will affect the performance of the organisms and the body. The body may influence the mind, but it is the mind that will control the body through the impulses brought about by the blood cells and the neuron cells.

---

[14] Wikipedia, "Neuron", http://en.wikipedia.org/wiki/Neuron.

DISTRIBUTION OF PLASMA AND RESOURCE

Power distribution

The 'digestive system' will produce the power source, plasma, the body will be using. The energy source, power supply and fuel, will provide the matter that will enable the mechanisms and motor areas to evolve and perform. Instructions through the plasma/blood will be by impulses; instructions through the plasma are mechanical, reflexive reaction. The amount of blood, the amount of protein in the blood, the masses in the blood, the energy in directing the force to do work, and the timing will affect the reflexive reaction.

The plasma cells provide energy source and masses of matter to motor areas through the blood vessels. The plasma cells will direct instructions to areas by impulse. The impulse is the amount of force caused by the amount of cellular mass causing force to do work. The different masses of protein cells in the plasma are known as hormones and adrenalines. All motor areas and mechanisms/organs are connected to each other by blood vessels.

The body will grow. The mechanisms and motor areas will grow along. To enable this, the matrix of the blood vessels will grow more complex. All areas and mechanisms will expand and 'learn' how to perform in coordination with each other. All areas must have some purpose in the body. The cell will contribute to the body by contributing to each other. Even if certain areas have no direct contact with each other, the mechanics of the impulse and reflexive reaction will keep them in cooperation with each other; each area and each station will be incorporated into the anatomy (autonomy) of the animal body (human body).

Resource distribution / usage of blood cells

As the cell travels through the blood vessels, the blood will deliver protein (masses of matter) for the mechanism and motor area to reproduce, develop and do its job. To do work, the motor area and/or mechanism may have to expand or contract. The protein sources will enable the change in the mechanisms and motor areas causing impulses and reflexive reaction.

> *ie. As the arm lifts up, the blood vessels of the areas will cause the areas to expand and contract to enable the limb to maneuver.*

The protein is the refined source in the blood that will stimulate the organisms, the mechanisms and motor areas, to reproduce and develop. As the organism grows or changes form, the route of the blood vessel will change affecting the impulse in the blood vessel. Some organisms will add to the momentum in the blood that will trigger reflexive reactions by other organisms.

The generics, genetics, of the cells will influence the growth and form of the organism. The growth and forming of the organism will affect the usage of the proteins and masses of matter in the blood cells. The higher the metabolism, the more proteins and masses of matter in the cells will be used. The organism will evolve and develop to use the proteins and masses of matter in the cells as intended by the metabolism.

> *ie. The higher the metabolism, the more energetic the person will be. The organisms will develop to use the protein and the sources in the blood.*

> *Ie. The more work to be done by the autonomous body, the more complex the organic body must become. The more complex the organism, more power source and masses of matter will be used. The more nutrient used, the higher the metabolism.*

Energy and force to do work will be provided by the organism through impulse enabled by the formation and development of the organism. The blood flow is a factor in the impulse in the blood flow directed to the next organism. The development and formation of the organism will direct the flow of the blood. The impulse from the blood flow will provide the impression on how the area and group of organisms will reflexively react. The more work the organism(s) have to do, the better reproduced and developed the organism(s) must be.

The organisms must keep in motion and operating at all times to keep the blood flowing, keep the blood circulating, and enrich the organisms. The organisms must evolve and develop. The blood cells will provide the masses of matter to be used by the organisms to reproduce and develop. As the organism reproduces and develops, it sets off impulses to direct other organisms to react in reflex. Consistent motion by the body cells and its organisms will provide the impulses and the rich blood supplies fellow organisms will need.

CONTROL OF THE BLOOD FLOW AND ORGANISMS BY THE NERVES

The nerves give detailed instructions to the organisms to operate and cause an impulse leading to a reflexive reaction. The neurons are cells in the nerves. Messages/instructions are relayed through the neurons. The instructions are by levels of electrical charges that are relayed through the neurons. Organisms will have sensory capacity(s).

Organisms will enable:
Audio: **hearing and speaking;**
Visual: **sight;**
Gustatory: **taste;**
Olfactory: **smell;**
Somatic: **touch and feel.**

The organisms are trained to respond to the sense(s). With responding, an impulse of electrical signal will travel from neuron to neuron to reach the central network control, the Central Nervous System (the CNS)[15]. The frequency of the energy signal, the power level of the charge, will identify which organism the signal came from, and for what type of sensory. The size of the charge will identify what has occurred in the area, physically. The CNS in the motor area known as the cranium will react automatically or by control.

---

[15] Wikipedia, "Central Nervous System", http://en.wikipedia.org/wiki/Central_nervous_system.

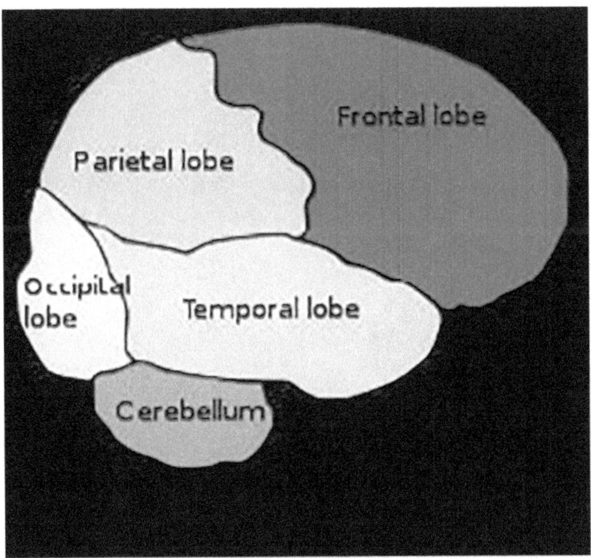

Fig. 9[16]

The cranium consists of several lobes. The lobe simulates a complex processing station with many towers that consist of many outlets and connections. These stations and towers have much memory areas for work and storage. Each lobe is directed to specific sensory and sensory reaction. The lobes will be intertwined with each other by a complex matrix of nerves, the neural network. The lobes and the organisms with the specific sensory will have been trained and preprogrammed to react to specific circumstances that cause specific sensory reflex and impulse reaction(s). A central processor will process all data from the different lobes to determine if the CNS is to react automatically by previous memories, or be evaluated by the mind that is hosted by the cranium cortex. [17]

[16] Wikipedia, "Lobes of the Brain," http://en.wikipedia.org/wiki/Lobes_of_the_brain.

[17] Wikipedia, "Human Brain", http://en.wikipedia.org/wiki/Human_brain.

Physiological Network

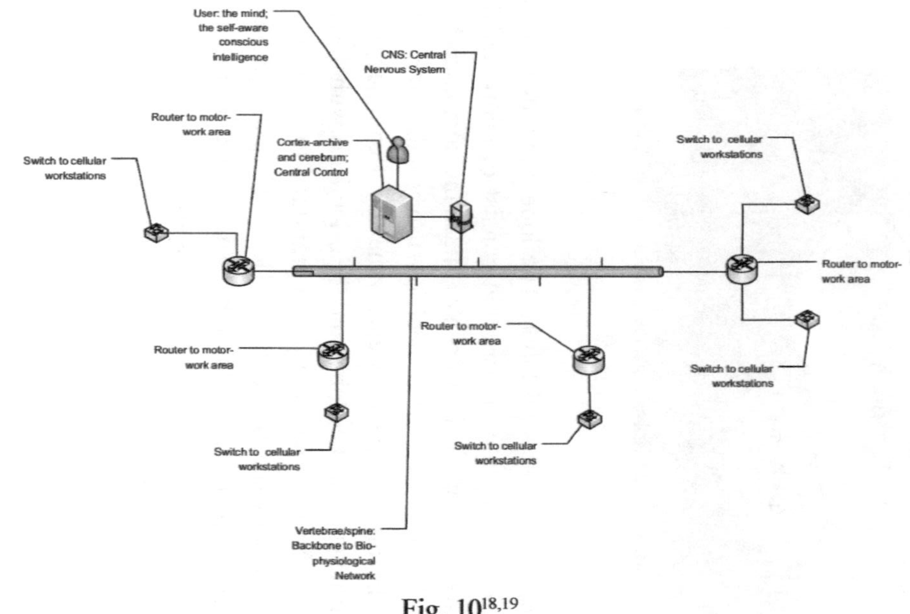

Fig. 10[18,19]

---

[18] The network matrix of a nervous network system is similar to a cybernetic network system and has been constructed by the Visio 2007 program.

All cybernetic mechanical devices are now carbon based mechanical devices (organisms).

[19] The power line (the blood vessels) is separate from the nervous system line (nerves); but they travel along the same path way.

Physiological Flow Chart

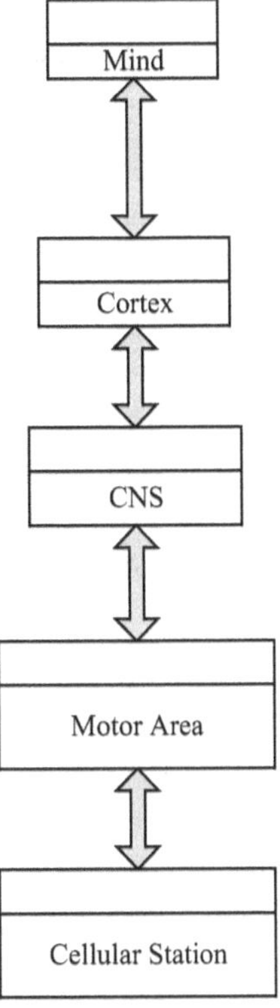

Fig. 11 [20]

The more work the cranial motor has to do to process and develop the information obtained from the sensory in the organisms of the body, the more energy and work force the cranial motor will need. The cranial motor and its neural matrix must be reproduced and developed well to do much work of processing.

---

[20] The flow chart of network matrix of the cellular organisms has been constructed on the Visio 2007 program.

The self-aware conscious intelligence is the mind and the person residing in the body.

The cortex holds the long term memories of the experiences to be used again.

The CNS directs all messages from the motor areas of the body to the cortex and vice versa.

Each motor area relays messages from the CNS to the to the cellular stations and vice versa.

The higher the quality of the neuron cells in the neural matrix, the better relaying of electrical impulses and message delivery for processing. The cranium and the organisms of the body will have been trained well in reacting to the blood impulses and the electrical impulses through time. The mind and administrative user of the cranium and its lobes will have been trained to interpret the impulses processed and gathered from the different lobes. The mind is not tangible so it will interpret and react to the processed data intangibly (psychologically).

The better built the organisms, neuron cells, and the nerve lining, the more efficient the nerve line will be in sending/delivering the electrical impulses and instructions. The weaker the organisms, neurons cells and nerve lining, the greater the chance of suspension of action or shut down in the nerve circuit and neural circuit during a sudden sensory reaction.

> *ie. The body will have learned what it has smelled, tasted, seen, heard, and felt, and how it will react to it.*

> *ie. The CNS will relay signals amongst the organisms incorporated into the autonomous body automatically as pre-trained to unless the experience is beyond pretraining.*

> *ie. The mind of the person will decide how the body will react toward situations that affect such sensory behaviors.*

BIOLOGICAL DEFICIENCY

Deficiency in Nutrient

Fuel, blood, is refined from the resources from the external environment. The raw resources will provide the nutrients that will produce energy source and masses of matter to be used by the organisms in the body. The higher the nutrient content (quatlity and quantity), the richer the proteins will be in the cells of the plasma. This will enable the organism(s) to reproduce and develop for more complex operations. As the raw resources (food) diminish in quantity and/or quality, the quantity and quality of the energy source and matter in the blood cells will diminish. The reproduction and development of the organisms will diminish. The body will become weak.

Stage 1: ***Trafficking and gathering of nutrient from resources diminishes and is suspended.***

Deficiency in Production and Distribution

The food is refined into plasma and fuel to be used by the organisms in the body. No matter how rich in quantity and/or quality the nutrition and nutrient may be in the food supply, if the energy source and masses of matter in the blood is not sufficient, the blood will still be weak and the organisms will not be developing properly. The organisms will not be performing as well as intended for the region and the body. Factor VIII and above in the plasma will enable the blood to be dense and not 'pour out' like water when the blood vessel or body is breached. Factor VII in the plasma will enable the blood to provide the necessary protein to the skins to repair themselves faster. The blood and the skin will work together to seal the wound.

If the person's body is producing blood with deficiency in Factor VIII or above, the person has hemophilia. The blood will start pouring out fast. Because the blood is thin, it will not carry enough energy source and masses of matter to the organisms for them to reproduce and develop fast and productively. The skin cannot seal the wound, breached area, fast enough without assistance of the protein from the blood.

A person with Factor VII Deficiency will bleed continuously until the wound is blocked or sealed. In an external surface wound, the wound will be noticed. Aid will be provided before something severe occurs. Until the wound is sealed and stops bleeding, there will be pain. The wound may not kill, but the pain will be annoying. In an internal wound, the wound will not be noticed. Until the annoying pain is noticed, no assistance will be provided. Continuous bleeding can lead to much loss of blood and damage to the body. Untreated internal bleeding can be damaging. With the lack of blood, the organisms will diminish in reproduction and development. The body will become very weak.

The lower the quality and/or quantity of power source and matter source from the nutrient, the weaker the blood cells. Impulse of the blood cells will be slow and weak.

Stage 2:   ***Trading and distribution of product amongst the organisms and regions diminishes and is suspended.***

Deficiency in the Nervous Network

The organisms of the body are linked together by their power line called the blood vessel. The blood cells, plasma, provide the nutrient and protein in the energy source and the masses of matter to be used by the organism to reproduce, develop, and operate. The development and formation of the organisms will affect the momentum of the blood flow, bringing about impulses. To manipulate the organism(s) to react to electrical charge, neuron cells will direct energy charge to the organism(s). The neurons will travel in the nervous network relaying electrical charges through the nervous system.

Organisms have specific senses. Sensory reaction will be directed back to the CNS and the lobes in the cranium. In processing the senses, much work will be done by the cranium motor area. This will require much work energy. Much power will be used. While processing, memory space, work space, will be needed. The more work the lobes and primary processor have to do; the more memory/work space will be used. Concentration on one area of work will direct all efforts away from the other work. If one sensory system is diminishing, much energy will be 'wasted' in attempt to revive this sensory. Because much or all efforts are concentrating on this sensory, the cranial lobes will lose concentration in the other parts of the body. The circuit line will weaken and possibly crash, in the nervous network in the body, or the neural network in the cranium. The body will go in to seizure in the cranium or seizure in the body.

If the structure of the body has been damaged during construction, or due to an accident, the person will have a hard time keeping the body in control. Communication between the organism(s) and the CNS and its lobes will be strained to the point of suspension. The body will be in chaos until order through the communication system, the nervous system, is restored. All non essential operations will have to be suspended to save energy and matter source for the nerves and the cranial motor.

Stage 3:   ***Communication and direction for order and restoration is suspended.***

BIO-ORGANIC MATRIX

The matrix of an organism simulates the matrix of a non-organism to the minute details; the android body simulates the human body down to the finest details and operational capacity. An android is a non-organism. It cannot respond to stimuli and reproduce and develop on its own. Reproduction and development, to adjust to adapt, can only be done by external assistance. A human body is an organism. It can respond to stimuli and reproduce and develop, adjust and adapt, on its own.

The object lying on the table simulates to the object that was previously dissected on the same table. It has four limbs (two legs and two arms); and has a part extending out of the main body. This part will be identified as the head containing a central network control called a cranium, or brain.

Like an android, the human body functions like an autonomous machinery consisting of a matrix of many sub-machineries. The autonomous machinery will locate and transport raw resources to the body. There will be sub-machineries (internal machineries) that will receive and process the raw resources. Compounds in the raw resources (food) will provide the means to produce the energy source and masses of matter at the level the internal machineries can use. The machineries will be designed and positioned in the autonomous matrix to maintain this autonomy, anatomy. The power lines, blood vessels, passing through the machineries will link the machineries to each other setting communication by the free flow of sources traveling through the power lines. The size level of source(s) and the amount of the source(s) traveling through the power lines will determine the impulses and the type of reflexive reaction that will occur. Along with energy source and matter source, hormone masses will also travel along in the power lines, blood vessels. There must be free flow of power blood/plasma, through the blood vessels and the machineries (organs) for communication and operation to take place.

There must be free flow through the blood vessels for the sources in the blood to be shared and used. The blood and sources will provide the means for mechanisms, organs, to reproduce and develop. In reproducing and developing, the organ(s) will be reconstructed to deliver the blood in different ways affecting the reflexive reactions. Each mechanism has its memory capacity to operate accordingly. In an organism, an organ has the capability to reproduce and develop to operate on its own until the cranium decides otherwise. Whether or not there is any instruction from the cranium, the organs and the mechanical area will respond to the situation by reflexive reaction as they were preprogrammed to, trained to. If reflexive reaction causes disruption in the free flow, there can be buildup of power and matter or lack of power and matter. With little to lack of control of the power line and the matrix, order will have been seized or taken away (seizure).

Another form of communication is by direct message from the cranium through the nervous system, nerves. Instead of providing energy source or matter source, minute mass will stimulate reaction that will trigger the organ to operate in such ways that will affect the impulse in the free flow in the power line affecting the reflexive reaction. The cranium will send signals through the nerves by electrical impulses through the minute masses present. The quality of the electrical impulse and the amount of the electrical impulse will determine the signal(s) that is being sent and received. Each organ has been constructed to receive, interpret, and react to the electrical signal sent through the nervous system. Data from the senses in the motor area will stimulate the area and the electrical signals in the nervous system. If the nervous system is delivering improper signals (electrical signals through bytes called neuron cells), the organs and/or motor areas can react improperly because they have not been trained and prepared for this. Order in reflexive reaction will have been seized or taken away (seizure) until order in the power line and the nervous system will have been restored.

To maintain free flow, all machineries and motor operations must keep active. If there is no free flow, the sources of power and matter will build up or drop down. The entire autonomous body will tire up and slow down in motion. Seizure can be due to build up of sources of power and masses. When an area or operation demands too much power and matter, the supply of sources can be drained, or can be selfishly dominated by that one area or operation.

Humans learn through his 5 physical senses; audio, visual, gustatory, olfactory, and somatic. If the visual/optical sensory(s) are defective and requires much power and matter to maintain and operate them, other areas will be denied of the needed sources. Exhaustion will occur. Massive seizure would lead to convulsion. If the motors and machineries are not prepared to operate at low level of power supply, the matrix will go into convulsion. With time, the matrix will learn to operate with little source supply. Seizure would just be suspended operation until restoration is done.

A nutrient is the energy source and masses of matter used by the carbon based organism called humans. It is produced from the raw resources called nutrition, food. The level and quality of the nutrient supply is determined by the quality of the nutrition provided by the external environment and the quality of the machineries (organs) that are processing the food. No matter how high in quality the nutrition may be, if the organs cannot produce the high quality of power source and matter source for the matrix to use, this autonomous human body will tire and weaken fast.

The energy and masses of matter in the blood will provide the means for the organisms and motor areas of the human body to reproduce and develop in activity and operation on their own. The organs, the internal machineries of the human organism, must be constructed and positioned properly to ensure free flow and proper momentum and operation. A rich quality of energy source and masses of mater in the blood will assist the organisms well. Nutrients provide the sources for the construction. Physics and mechanics by the coherent momentum of the matrix body will set the design for what is to be constructed.

Blood will provide the energy source and masses of matter to organs and areas to repair damage. The human body is an organism because the human body can respond to stimuli with reproduction and development. The condition the organism or area is in, the energy source and masses of matter are factors of the blood and stimuli affecting the response by the organism.

Blood provides the sources for reproduction and development. Cellular protection (white blood cell) is by reproduction and development. Leukocytes are the immune white blood cells that provide protection by defeating the invading cells and virus. All organs will reproduce and develop to evolve. No organ goes into full function once it has been produced. It will take time to develop into the stage where it can confront its duties at full capacity efficiently. As a cell, organ, area, or body grow, the others will grow along with it. They must evolve coherently together. If they do not evolve together, there will be a conflict with each other. This is uncontrolled growth, cancer.

POWER PRODUCTION: BLOOD FLOW

Blood is the power supply and store of energy to enable each area (each organ) to function. If they function properly, they will operate coherently with each other; the organs will operate coherently with each other. The blood must travel freely amongst the organs. If something happens causing the blood not to flow freely in the body, the buildup of power and blood in one location will convulsions and/or disorders in the body. This is seizure; control is taken away. Control through the communication network, the nervous system, has not been taken away here. It is orderly control and coherency by reflexive reaction that has been taken away.

When the gravitational field has been lost, coherency by reflexive reaction in the animal body will suspended. The animal body from Earth has been accustomed to gravitational acceleration, 9.82 m/s^2. Anything heavier or lighter than that, the body will be in chaos.

Engineer's Log: Lt. Cmd. Mat: 22200930

> "During the loss of gravity after the turbulence in Quadrant A occurred, there was a sudden loss of gravity. Objects that were not locked by magnetism or tied down drifted out of position. The power lines and the communication lines were tightly locked into place so they did not drift out of position. The only problem was the energy packets that delivered power through the power lines and the communication lines were to move freely. Loss of gravity resulted in the disruption in the flow of energy packets. This resulted in loss of power in certain areas, and distortion in the communication messages. The network of station consoles was in a moment of chaos until the

operational program of each station console was restored to operate on its own without the bridge and the CNC."

Doctor's Log: Cmd. Carl: 22200930

"Cadets in the Academy have been trained to go through anti-gravitational field training; they were required to experience anti-gravitational environment. Before going into the environment, they were prepared of it. Even prepared, cadets have reported feeling 'sick to their stomach' and need time to adapt to the anti-gravitational environment, and back again. The free flow of the cellular compounds in the blood lines must have been disrupted. The organs must have been operating out of order and incoherently with each other. The travels of the cellular compounds in the communication lines must have gone off route. This would make any person sick and confused."

"When the wave turbulence struck the Jonathan by surprise, the loss of the gravitational field was sudden. Nobody was prepared for the surprise. People drifted out their posts/stations and reported feeling sick. People returned back to their posts when gravitation was restored, but they were still sick."

"Surprise drills for loss of gravitational field must be prepared. People must learn to continue at their posts even when gravity has been lost. They must learn to adapt and find means to keep the stations operating even if the stations are cut off from the bridge or the crew man is forced off the console."

Captain's Log: Capt. Jameson: 22200930

"It has been about a week since we entered into Quadrant A and encountered the sudden turbulence. The crew and the vessel have still not recovered for the sudden surprise. Cmd. Johns have been instructed to work with all the departments to set up drills for the crew to adapt to the long space travel we will be doing. In doing so, the operational program at each station console and the work memory there must be prepared to operate on its own by the local crewmember's prepared instructions. We cannot move on until we are prepared. I want this ship (vessel and crew) to operate as a research ship fully prepared for diplomatic actions and defense by 22201031."

STRUCTURAL DEVELOPMENT

The Jonathan is a finely designed vessel. It is a new class of vessel for a new class of engines for newly found power that can deliver vessels great distances. This engine and new source of power is going to be tested now in Jonathan's maiden voyage into star systems far from the presently known star system we are in.

The construction of the vessel body begins in the 'dry dock'. As it is being constructed, its features are being made known to the newly organized crew. After the vessel's early stage of construction, construction of the surface body with the power line and the communication line laid into place, this vessel is ready to come out of the protected space and protected home star system.

The next stage of construction and development begins now as the Jonathan goes into Quadrant A through the quantum tunnel it creates from its engine. When the Jonathan encountered its first turbulence, the ship learns that it must develop new features to prepare for and hopefully avoid the problems that resulted. In doing so, surface structures, internally and externally, had to be changed. The outer hull of the vessel had to be adjusted to make the hyper tunnel and travel through the hyper tunnel more smoothly.

During the 20th Century and the 21st Century, the surface of the fuselage had to be smooth. The smoothness of the fuselage enabled a smooth sound barrier and tunnel to be created from the thrust of the plane. If the surface of the fuselage was not smooth, the plane would have created its own turbulence in the air.

Engineer's Log: Lt. Cmd. Mat: 22201010

"We went rolling with the wave. We had just came to full stop as we entered Quadrant A. The travel through the tunnel went safely. It could have been smoother and faster if the hull was smoother. Our engine creates the power to create the quantum barrier around the vessel, and the quantum tunnel travels far through. The barrier and the tunnel are created in accordance to the shape of the vessel. If the surface of the hull was smoother, the barrier and the tunnel pathway would have been smoother and faster with little to no disturbance."

"The wave struck us on the port side as we came to a full stop after a moment of impulse propulsion when leaving the hyper tunnel. Because the vessel was not flat or pointed on the side, a mass force striking a mass object that is wide caused a massive turbulent effect. It has come to the conclusion that all sides of the vessel must be flat sharp. The vessel can be oval shaped pointing forward like an egg, or flat sharp like a flat plate or saucer. This flat or sharp vessel can cut through mass with no disturbance. There is no mass in space. The hyper space in the hyper tunnel the vessel has created to travel through has mass. The sharper the vessel, the smoother and faster the vessel will travel."

"The adjustment(s) of the outer hull of the Jonathan has begun. A full construction of the vessel will have to be done at port. We will try the best to the create effects of a flat saucer around the vessel. This vessel is already saucer rounded but is not flat sharp. We will try to create this flat saucer effect with energy pushing the quantum barrier all around the vessel outward horizontally; on the starboard, aft, port, and front of the vessel. The barrier at the top and bottom of the vessel will be kept the same. The vessel will cut through mass in the hyper space without disturbance."

> "As we made attempts to create the saucer effect outside
> of the vessel, quarters had to be changed or constructed.
> Energy stations had to be placed into proper positions to
> manipulate the quantum barrier to create the saucer effect
> around the vessel. Realignments of the power lines and
> the communication lines have to be made."

The body of the Homo Sapient Erectus had a rounded body on the side. As this specie erected, stepped upward, his body pointed upward. The body was stretched wide vertically. Even though his body was rounded on the side enabling the air to travel around it on the side, the body of the Homo Sapient Erectus still encountered turbulence. He learned to bend forward to cut through the air mass. As he thrusts his body forward from the rear, he will face minor turbulent effects. His body will learn to shift internal mass to different positions to maintain buoyance in the speed tunnel he has created to travel through mass surrounding the tunnel.

As the outer body of the Homo Sapient Erectus evolved, his inner body evolved along to support the outer features. The architectural shape of his body will have to enable air mass to travel around the body. The muscles around the skeletal frame work of the body will enable this feature. The organs in the body will produce the necessary compounds to construct the muscles for a tall, strong rounded body. The blood vessels (the power line) and the nervous system (the communication line) will enable the organs (the quarters and facilities) to work coherently with each other.

The Homo Sapient Erectus learned to clothe his body to create temporary features; a sharp round body that enables the encountering air mass or water mass to go smoothly around the body. He builds his body to adapt to the environment he is in. If the environment he is going to encounter is going to vary from light to heavy, his body must learn to adapt. As he enters into a different environment, he will be clothed with protection. The longer he stays in this environment, the more adaptive and evolved his body will become. He will be able to stay in this environment without protective clothing around his body.

Doctor's Log: Cmd. Carl: 22201020

"Long travel in space will cause great effect on a crewmember's body. He has learned to adapt to long stays in space; long stays in an orbiting space station. The gravitational environment on board the Jonathan will be programmed for gravitational acceleration, 9.8 m/s^2. From time to time, crewmen will have to leave this gravitational environment and enter a different environment."

"After that moment with brief loss of gravity, people reported that they were struck with surprise and the body got sick. The Captain and the seniors agreed that everybody, including themselves, must learn to adapt to sudden loss if gravity but still continue moving. There will be difficulties, but the body must learn to adapt. With continuous training and drills for heavy environments and light environments, the body will evolve and develop ways to adapt to the change."

"The organs, muscles, blood vessels and nervous system within the body must get use to heavy environments and light environments. The surface of the body will develop new features. The body will evolve to adapt. By the time we return to Earth, how noticeable will the changes to our physical body be?"

NEURAL GUIDANCE

Each individual is responsible for his own task. At times, he will need the assistance of others. Communication network enables individuals to communicate with each other and provide assistance to each other. The telephone, now the computer network, has 'made the world smaller'.

The computer network, the IT, made communication amongst individuals all over the mass vessel (the world) convenient. In the 21st Century, mass traffic of messages on the IT and growing sophisticated programs had begun to make usage of the computer network difficult. The IT consisted of many different browser corporations that that had only the responsibility to provide only commercial information. Soon, the idea of the 'Cloud Computing' came to existence. The 'Cloud Computing' consisted of a large server processor and a large hard drive archive of program files. The 'Cloud Computing' becomes a large computer. This large processor will maintain traffic order by having requests for global files and massively used programs to be provided to all who are in request for them. Each computer console will serve as part of the RAM. The RAM, the processor and the hard drive at each individual console will serve as one. It will serve as one service memory in a large massive operational memory in a large computer (the Cloud Computing network).

The CNC is the primary processor on board of the vessel. The CNC is connected to a large RAM consisting of many pieces (station consoles). The CNC holds a large archive of program files and stored files to be used by the individual(s) at the station console(s).

Engineer's Log: Lt. Cmd. Mat: 22201015

> "We have been in Quadrant A for several weeks. We have designed and built new facilities and areas to reshape the

quantum barrier around the vessel. New power lines to power the stations, and new communication lines to link the stations with the mass computer of the vessel has been built. However the areas are built and stations are placed will affect how sensor signals will be received and interpreted. The vessel's computer, with the CNC, will direct each station how the vessel is to perform or respond. The vessel's computer will give instructions as preempted (as intended). If the situation is not preempted, or expected, the bridge will give the last minute orders. If the bridge's orders do not arrive fast enough, the crewmember at the station will give the last minute order."

"The Jonathan is changing. The stations and areas must develop new procedures to work coherently with each other. Each station will be programmed to operate by regular routine and expected operational procedures as planned. The vessel will respond to turbulence or sudden change to maintain buoyancy and safety. All stations will work coherently with each other. The CNC will instruct a plan of operation to a station. The surge of power and movement will cause other stations and areas to respond by reflexive response without the vessel's computer having to give detailed instructions to each station."

"We have been through repeated drills. Each station and each crewmember had to be trained and programmed to operate each console at each location automatically and maintain order without waiting for instructions. They will maintain at their position(s) and will respond reflexively unless instructions from the bridge or the crewmen are given."

Communication Officer's Log: Lt. Cmd. James: 22201015

"Engineering has reported that new stations and new lines have been put to place. To test if the stations are operating coherently with each other and with the vessel computer, the vessel will be put into fast impulse speed toward the sun. The gravitational force will cause turbulence. Tactical plans of operation for each station have been installed into each station console; how each console will operate at each location in accordance to the flight and operational plan will be carried out. Along with reflexive reaction by power and momentum, each station will link up with the CNC and vessel computer."

"Travelling into turbulence, unplanned for occurrence will be expected. The bridge will have to give instructions, detailed if necessary, to each station and to each area. The Jonathan will have to ride along with the turbulence's path, or ride into the turbulence. Internal locations inside the vessel will not be clear on what to do or what to expect. They will have to trust the bridge to give them instructions."

"Audio, visual and somatic sensory will receive data in accordance to how the station has been constructed and where they are placed. They will give these data to the CNC, the brain stem of the vessel's computer. The CNC will process the incoming data in accordance to the files and programs it has been stored and prepared with. If the gathered data processed are unprecedented, the computer will inform the bridge and request for instructions from the bridge."

Doctor's Log: Cmd. Carl 22201015

"The crewmen are learning to adapt. To adapt to the light environments and heavy environments, the bodies are expected to change. They may or may not be noticeable by regular eye sight but their internal features will change. In an intended motion, the mind will instruct the body to act through the brain stem. Because this is going to be a new experience with no plan(s) prepared, the mind will have to give detailed instructions on what to do and how to respond."

"The crew has not gotten used to a light or anti-gravity environment. A crewmember has realized that he needs to grab a floating object. He will have to give instruction to his right arm to stretch out to the object. Reaching near the object, he gives instructions for e fingers in his right hand to stretch out and grab the gear."

"In attempting to reach out and grab the object, a ball, the brain stem instructs the right shoulder to move in a certain way. When the shoulder began to act as instructed, the rest of the arm reacted reflexively in accordance to the external interference(s) and the internal interference(s)."

"The first time a person, a child, has a baseball thrown at him, the ball strikes his chest because he hasn't learned to raise his hand fast enough and move his body into position to catch the ball. In a next few tries, the mind and brain stem give instructions for different plans of movement by the body, the arm and the hand to catch the ball at different paths and positions. With time, the brain stem only needs to give a speculation on what is coming, where it is headed and where it may strike. With pre-planned procedures, all parts of the body will operate coherently with each other by reflexive response."

EFFECT ON STRUCTURE AND GUIDANCE SYSTEM

Power produced will provide the energy to operate. Power delivered in energy packets will provide means to produce resources for life support and construction (renovation). Damages can be repaired; renovation and development of the structure can be carried out. Communication is delivered in energy packets separate from the packets delivering power. Both types of packets must circulate throughout the structure from device (station) to device (station).

The structure will operate autonomously when all areas and all stations operate coherently. Should this structure shift position adapt to the situation, all areas and all stations must adapt along. For a sudden change, certain stations will need more power than others. To maintain strength after the change, the structure must eventually have all stations and areas operating sharing power and resources equally again.

Deficiencies may occur with time. Should any area have difficulty operating to full capacity, don't waste energy and strain the communication system (the sensory system) and operational system. Reassign the duties and responsibilities to other locations, and re-direct the power and sensory to them. Keep the structure (the vessel) in balance. Maintain the balance of power and resources; balance the operation and distribute the power and resources properly where are needed.

To enable all stations to operate coherently with each other, a Cloud Computing exists to have all station consoles form one massive computer. The central processor, and brain stem, of the large computer will control the control and trafficking of the messages in the mass network. All stations will communicate with each other, and work with each other through the 'brain stem'.

Engineer's Log: Lt. Cmd. Mat: 22201105

"We have advanced far since we entered into Quadrant A and begin refining ourselves. Our primary engine and secondary engine in excellent condition and do not need any fitting. We have produced enough power supplies for reconstruction and travel. Now that new consoles can be constructed, new wirings and quarters and facilities can be constructed. The hull can be refitted so that that external imagery by the quantum barrier around the hull can be formed. The hull will not be a flat saucer just as long that as the quantum barrier will form a flat saucer to travel through the quantum (hyper) tunnel and change position at any moment without any interference."

"Each station will need power for the console to operate and the local automaton to perform the necessary task(s). The crew will need nourishment and nutrients to operate. Nourishment will be provided by the supplemental food supplies grown from the gardens constructed on board the vessel. The power from the 1st Engine will provide the energy to operate the facilities. The crew and the stations can best operate in an acceptable gravitational field."

Communication Officer's Log: Lt. Cmd. James: 22201105

"Entering into Quadrant A, we encountered our first turbulence. Communications for sensory and operation were disrupted. We had to reprogram the stations to redirect the path of the power, the path of the communication, and the routine operation(s) of local station(s). New plans were constructed by trial and error. We have created temporary plans. New plans will be constructed with time and experiences."

"It is understood that the Cloud Computing becomes the computer of the ship (the crew and vessel). Each station is a piece of the RAM in the ship's computer. The RAM, CPU and hard drive (memory archive) of the station console.

The CNC is the CPU and brain stem to the ship's computer. The CNC is also connected to a massive memory archive."

"The RAM, the CPU and the archive at each station console will operate as one. They become one surface work memory that keep in operation at all times. The station's work memory will keep the routine operational memory of the location active. There will be large memory work memory space for much work to be done. Variables created from previous processing work can be kept for further processing work to be done. Formulated work memory file can be created to capture incoming data fast and store immediately created variables to be used immediately without delay. Work results will be fast."

"The ship's computer can store mass amount of incoming data and newly created variables from different stations to be stored for further usage by any station. All stations will work with each other coherently through the ship's computer (the ship's CNC brain stem and the ship's archive)."

"Keep the CNC processor active. The RAM must be active; each station console that makes up the RAM of the ship's computer must be kept active. The work memory (the local RAM, CPU and hard drive) of the station console must be kept active. The CNC and its ship's archive will keep the mass memory of data and constructed program files from the local station console. The local station console need only know its operation and keep up with it. Should the local station ever be suspended but no shut off, the station can easily restore to full capacity. If the CNC needs to send a message or relay a message from another station console, the CNC will send a message that only involves only that station console. Only that station console will be able to receive it. Should the energy charge of the message mistakenly also involve other console(s) with no direct intension, seizure will occur. The network will be in chaos resulting in suspension of operation resulting in erratic somatic actions (convulsions). The message charge may have been sent by the CNC, but it may have actually started from a message charge sent from other location(s) in the vessel body."

Doctor's Log: Cmd. Carl: 22201106

"Since entering Quadrant A, people have experienced injuries that required intensive care. Their bones and flesh bodies received damages. Like energy packets that carried power to locations to be used, cells served the same responsibility. If the blood cells are not carrying the sufficient quality or quantity of blood and nutrients required by the location(s), the energy packets are not carrying the sufficient quality or quantity of power to the location(s) that require the power. It has been found that one of my patients, crewmember 1112789299, has blood deficiency. He lacks a blood factor that provides strength to the energy packets, blood cells, from leaking out fast after a surface wound or damage. It appears that he has Factor 8 Deficiency (First Level of Hemophilia). He will have to be restricted from physical duties that can cause damage to the physical damage to the body. He must be assigned to stations where he only needs to sit by the console and manage it and maintain the location through the console without somatic movement."

"During the regular review of crew after the gravitational loss, medical history of crewmen that were once recorded came to service. Crewmember 1112789299's history of Factor 8 Deficiency was noticed. Lt. Cmd. 6606362082's history of Factor 7 Deficiency was also noticed. Factor 7 provides the protein factor to motor area (cellular area) to regenerate and repair damage at the area; the amount of power in the cellar power packet to be delivered to area station to repair damage(s). Lt. Cmd. 6606362082's condition is not noticeable until severe damage resulting in blood loss occurs. He is able to keep his post and station as long as he avoids severe damage (and blood loss)."

"1st Lt. 1967072720's medical record was excellent during the Academy and when he boarded the Jonathan. During the recent medical review of the crew, it was found that 1st Lt. 1967072720's blood and organs were not functioning properly. The cells were not regenerating as expected. The blood showed defect (illness). Damaged cells are expected to be replaced by the body with regenerated cells. The damaged blood cells were damaging the body faster than the clean body cells could be regenerated. Cancer has occurred. The cancer was in the blood. In the 20th Century, medical identified this virus in the blood and body as Leukemia. 1st Lt. 1967072720 is recognized as mentally, physically and academically fit for duty and does not need to be reassigned. But, he must go to the infirmary for medical reviews consistently."

"After that moment of loss of gravity, people reported of nervousness and stomach sickness. There was a person who reported of severe pain in his bones. This patient, crewmember 1966060434, was given a full review of his body. It was found that there were signs of weakness in his bones. He was given bone test(s) to confirm this. He was young but he has gradual osteoporosis. His bones are weakening. Weak gravity and heavy can shatter his bones. He must be treated with proper diets and exercises."

"One of my patients, crewmember 1966060445, showed signs of visual difficulties. He had a history of visual difficulties and needed eye wear. She can get unclear sighting without eye wear, and she will have no clear focus on what has been sighted. During the weeks we were at Quadrant A, she had to report to the infirmary of difficulties with her somatic responses, motion in balance. It appeared that she had relied too much on clear visual to guide her physical actions. She has to go through trainings to learn how to use all of her physical senses. She will have to train her Central Nervous System, brain stem, and all areas of her body to use all 5 physical senses in coordination. If one sensory shows signs of difficulties, the other senses will have to compensate. Certain areas will have to do more work than others. Blood and power source will have to be distributed and shared wisely. There must be no hoarding of blood and power, nor miss usage of blood and power. There must be coherency amongst the sensory and stations or the power will be wasted on unproductive results."

"The nervous system is the communication line in the animal body (human body). It delivers signals amongst the locations and motor areas to operate coherently. The CNS brain stem will receive the messages and traffic them to the other locations to have the entire body work autonomously. Messages will be sent through communication lines by energy packets (neuron cells). Messages will be by bursts of energy charges from cell to cell to location(s). Sensory is an operational program in each station console. If something stimulates one of the sensory, the station and location will respond with additional message charge(s) sent along the communication line to the brain stem (the CNC and the CNS). If the message charge through the communication line is out of balance or inaccurate resulting in incoherent responses by other stations and areas, this would result in seizure of neural control."

"One of the crew members, ensign 1966060412, was struck in the head when he fell once the gravitational field was restored. He was bruised badly in the left side resulting in much pain. He began to show reflexive reaction consistently even when nothing was touching the damaged side of his body. It shows that his somatic senses on the damaged side have become unstable. After treating him for his bad bruise, he was instructed to come back for further tests."

"One week after the bruise, this patient's body began to operate irregularly after a sharp pinch in his body by a pin. The body was in convulsion. The pinch from the pin stimulated his somatic sensory. It appeared that the message charge being sent to the CNS was not accurate. The CNS sent inaccurate message charges to the other locations around the body. The inaccuracy of the message charge resulted in seizure of control by the communication line; seizure in the nervous system. This disorder (seizure disorder) can be due to difficulty in location(s) of the body; or difficulty in the CNS."

"All operations in the body's areas and the cranium housing the CNS brain stem and the cortex (the archive) must be kept active. Even if suspended resulting in slowing of the brain and the areas, all area can restore to full capacity maybe not as effective as before. The training by experience has enabled all areas to act by reflexive intelligence without conscious awareness. The local station does not need to worry about the other station's responsibility(s); just keep concentration on local operations and how local operations will work coherently with the rest of the body."

"The more complex and coordinated the work the body will do and the brain will be responsible in managing, the more complex the communication network (the nervous system) will be. The network connection in the cranium, the bridge, will become complex also. The CNC processor and the cortex archive will be building more connections to enable more storage and more operations to be done. A large percentage of the cranium will be in operation. The CNC/CNS brain stem and the cortex archive will eventually evolve into one."

Counselor's Log: Lt. Cmd. Simmons: 22201107

"It has been a month since we left home port. It has been a month since this crew has encountered any humans other themselves. It is understandable that they will show nervousness and paranoia. People have reported of emotional stress and fear. The fear in the mind has led the brain and the CNS brain stem to misdirect the body to act irregularly."

"The CNC central processor (the CNS brain stem) and the primary archive (the cortex archive) will provide the general files and generic program plans (the plan of operation) that all station consoles will use. The station will be left the responsibility of constructing its own action plan by fitting the incoming data on to the known general program plan. The bridge (the cranium and brain) can only provide the overall strategy in confronting the situation. It is left to the local station (the local area in the body) to do what it can with what it is provided with. Each station will adapt and compensate with the variable data and the generic plan provided. All stations will work coherently with each other to maintain the autonomy of the body. The stations of the vessel body will have its simple operational program to work with, and work coherently with other stations in the body. The primary processor of the CNC or the CNS brain stem is intended to traffic guidance from the mind (the seniors on the bridge) to the stations in the vessel body. The brain stem will guide the stations in operating the body through complex procedures. If there is no bridge (a brain and mine), the stations will operate coherently together by the basic operational program that they were constructed by. They will operate coherently together but with no guidance and no purpose. The brain stem (the CNC processor) will only maintain the coherency amongst the stations. A functional body with no operational brain is no longer a person but a lifeless automaton or 'a dead zombie'."

"As implied by the Communication Officer and the Doctor, the brain stem at the bridge and the nerves all around the body must be kept active with all power (blood) kept circulating. All areas must be kept active. All nerves must be kept active. If kept active, all areas will be able to respond automatically by reflex without conscious awareness. All sub-conscious intelligence will concentrate on receiving incoming data and constructing new procedures in using the operations of the local station console. As the body and the brain evolve with time, the brain stem, the cortex archive and the nervous system will do even more work together. The brain will get more complex with more lining connections in the brain. Because the brain will be working harder, it will need more energy and power. The nervous system all around the body will be working harder so the nervous system and all areas will need more power and energy. The body will get tired until it has become stronger and have learned to use its resources conservatively and productively."

"The condition the area is in will determine how the vessel (the body) will gather its external data accordingly and deliver the info to the CNC and the bridge for reasoning. The CNC and the bridge (the seniors and the captain) will process the info as received. Fast or slow in coming up with the response does not determine that the ship's computer (the mind and brain of a person) is slow or impaired. The CNC must gather the info, process it, understand it, and create an efficient generic plan for all areas of the vessel body to work with. The ship's computer may appear to be slow; but when the ship's computer has created a generic operational plan, the ship and its computer will be extremely fast in getting future work done."

"Each individual is to concentrate only on its local operation(s) in accordance to the generic plan. The incoming data and info will fit into the generic plan, constructing the immediate plan of action for the location. No extreme thinking needs to be done. Just let the bridge do the thinking and the stations do the working."

"The primary processor in the vessel body, the CNC and brain, will use the most energy to maintain order on board the vessel. Every area will have to work hard to maintain the power-cellular packets, and the communication-cellular packets, to keep circulating. Every area must work coherently with each other and use the resources provided fairly. If there is internal conflict, the ship (the vessel and the crew) will be in chaos. If the ship begins to use more than it has, it will begin to get exhausted. The ship must be conservative with its resources."

"Because nobody was trained or prepared for such a deep space voyage out of hibernation, people were in fear and paranoid. They were willing to release their tensions on anything, even on fellow crew members. Violence almost resulted. It has been a month of solitude for the crew as a whole. But, the crew members have shown support for each other. Once an efficient generic plan has been constructed to encourage all to feel comfortable at their stations and in this voyage, the crew will feel confident in themselves and this ship's mission."

"Luckily, the Captain had decided that the Jonathan will avoid contact with any sentient beings and planetary contacts in Quadrant A. The main goal of our stay in Quadrant A for the first month is learning what the Jonathan has, what the crew has, what fittings need to be made, and what kind of general action plans that can be formulated for future purposes."

Science Officer's Log: Lt. Cmd. Kevin: 22201107

"Neutrinos are produced from decay of mass. We have learned how to manipulate the positioning of the amount of specific masses to be destroyed (decayed) to produce the amounts of specific neutrinos. In doing so, we manipulate further production of mass and power. In doing so, we have learned how to manipulate the delivery of massive power, and delivery of message signals by energy charges."

"We have learned to decay mass and manipulate the production of energy and power by light speed at variables instead of constant. As the Homo Sapient Erectus (Man) evolves and uses his cranium (the cortex archive and CNS brain stem) more productively, he will learn to manipulate the decay of mass and production of neutrinos accordingly to control mass and energy."

"With our knowledge of neutrino production at the moment, we can produce the resources we need for fitting and reconstruction. We can manipulate the necessary power to produce the needed food supplements our bodies need. The externally produced neutrinos, power and mass can provide assistance to crew members to repair their damaged body(s)."

"As we refit our vessel, we can spend time to develop a plan on how to relate with our species and cultures. We are about to move on to the next quadrant in our journey. On 2221110, we will create the quantum hyper-tunnel to travel into Quadrant B. We will observe deeply our production of power and usage of power inside and outside of the quantum hyper-tunnel."

"The Homo Sapient Erectus (Man) evolved from a wild animal, the wild primate. After learning how to capture fire and use it, he began to advance and has advanced far. He was traveling through the forest with his limbs yesterday; now he is traveling through the stars using quantum power. Even reaching this far, Man is still housed in an animal body and is prone to submit to his animal instincts."

Executive Officer's Log: Cmd. Johns: 22201107

"As administrator of protocol, I am responsible for assigning the crew to their posts and observe their performance. I am to work with the Security Officer and the Staff Officer to learn how the crew is adapting to the operational plan and the action plans chosen. The Staff Officer is to report to me about the crew's social and psychological attitudes. The Security Officer is to report to me about any discrepancy(s) that has occurred or may occur. I am to insure that the Security Officer will maintain secure order peacefully and diplomatically and not encourage any further discrepancy(s)."

"While in Quadrant A, Lt. Mans has informed to me that the crew is nervous with paranoia. They need training and encouragement for deep space voyage such as this. Crew members have been reported with damage to the bodies after the loss of gravity. Cmd. Carl has informed me that a crew member has gotten seizure disorder due to damage to the body and nervous system. A crew member has been reported having lack of coordination due to deficiency in one of the senses, visual. He has to learn to use all of senses. A crew member has been found with blood deficiency and will need treatment and must be assigned to a new post."

"Lt. Cmd. Xiao reported that crew members were near violent discrepancy(s) due to fear and paranoia. Order was restored calmly without bringing any attention to the difficulty."

"I am the administrative officer. I must make sure that the details of the internal conditions of the ship (the crew and the vessel) are satisfactory. If the ship does not have to make any changes, I will handle the problem on my own. If the situation is not minor and will require the entire ship to make adjustments, it is my responsibility to report the situation to the Captain and make suggestions from the suggestions proposed by the seniors. It is I who will report to the Captain directly; nobody is to go above me. A brief report will be provided for the Captain."

Captain's Log: Captain Jameson: 22201107

"I trust Cmd. Johns will take care of the crew wisely. He has done well during our stay in Quadrant A. The rest of the seniors have advised Cmd. Johns and me about how the ship (the crew and the vessel) must be refitted to continue our mission and journey. I will let my seniors and the ExO (Cmd. Johns) take care of the internals of the ship. I will concentrate on the ship's mission and the anomalies (planets, civilizations, space, etc.) we will encounter."

"In our first turbulence, we learned about the physical disturbances we will have to be prepared for in deep space. We will have to develop tactical plans of maneuvers to confront difficulties the vessel will encounter. The crew will need physical fitting and psychological fitting to adapt to long deep space voyage. We must be confident when we encounter new civilizations, and represent ourselves and the United Federation Star System diplomatically."

SOCIAL AUTONOMY

BUILDING BLOCK IN AN ORGANIZATION

Conception and plan for an organization

Organization is intangible. The true elements of an organization are both tangible and intangible. The tangible elements would be the physical resources, support(s) and trading credit(s) (funds and trade agreements) as provisions, to be used, traded and distributed. The personnel and staff in operating the organization are tangible. The intangible elements consist of trust, friendship, credits and trade agreements, and social conditions. These elements will form the structure, design and operation of the organization.

The elements of the organization must adapt with the elements of the external environment. The generic structure of the organization is by the way all similar organizations are constructed, developed, and have performed. The organization and its structure is by the ideology of a purpose that a party, one individual or a group of individuals insists on. The organization is the group and the purposes, the individual(s) are putting their efforts toward. Intangible source of social support and trade credits, and tangible source of materials and personnel, will be gathered externally to help the organization to operate.

Construction of the organization and its matrix in the operation

A physical exchange of supplies and personnel will be transferred from station to station, and department to department. Operation will require work to be done. The organization will be broken down into departments and operational areas. The purpose and operation of the area(s) form the structure of the organization. Each area will have its assignment and purpose. The different areas will be united by the purpose of the organization. Instead of having all areas/departments scattered around in chaos and different purposes, all will be confident with what they are doing and why they are doing it.

Supplies will enable work to be physically done. Social support of personnel and purpose of each team, and the purpose of the organization will encourage group effort. For the organization to operate efficiently, all areas and departments must operate efficiently. Provision, supplies of materials and social support to the organization and all its areas must be distributed amongst each other. The organization will require work and team effort. Supplies enable work; social support enables team effort. Funds (trade credits) are part of the provisions required to run the matrix.

Construction of the communication matrix

Tangible and intangible supplies will be exchanged amongst the departments of the organization. To maintain the usage of internal supplies efficiently, there must be social communication and support. The different areas must know how they will work with each other to ensure they are jointly productive and enable the organization to be productive. The different areas must communicate with each other for the purpose of the organization, not the wishes of a party of individual(s).

Trust and social support is intangible. All member(s) of the area and its team will communicate with each other to get the area's work done. All departments/areas will communicate with each other in trust and friendship to exchange support and supplies for the purpose and result of the organization.

> *Gathering of external resource is trafficking.*

> *Exchange of material supplies and social support in the organization is the distribution of supplies within. Trading is the impulse that will enable tangible work and intangible work to be done.*

Efforts to socialize and communicate amongst fellow members of the organization are communication and enables assistance and restoration to changes.

Funds will gather the external resources required, production of the internal provisions required, and the distribution of the provisions required by all areas of the matrix.

DEFICIENCIES IN THE SOCIAL STRUCTURE

Deficiency in Provisions

An organization is formed and exists by its internal infrastructure. The organization will set a rules of protocol that identifies who/what it is, how it operates, and how the divided sectors of the organization will work together to get the organization's job done. Along with the strong and confident infrastructure, the organization will require tangible resources to provide supplies and personnel to get the job done. The organization will also require intangible resources to provide support in the organization and its work efforts.

If there is limited or no supplies (no provisions), there will be little to no possibility to do the job. If there is limited or no personnel, who will get the job done? If there is limited or no social support, how will the organization find encouragement, funds and support to get the job done, or distribute the organization's work results and gather more support. If there is limited or no funding to support the organization, the organization will have limited or no means to get the supplies and personnel to get the job done; and limited to no means to promote the organization's plan to the public for social support.

Stage 1:   ***Sudden excitement has disturbed the gathering of tangible and intangible resources to get the job done; gathering of resources is diminishing or is suspended.***

Deficiency in Production and Trade/Distribution

Resources, tangible and intangible, have been obtained from outside of the company and organization. Social supports, finances, supplies, and information have been obtained. There is satisfaction and confidence that the organization with what it has obtained. To get the job properly and successfully done, all parts of the organization will have to get their shares of the resources obtained for proper usage. Each department will obtain and use the resources in accordance to the department's contribution to the organization's intended plan and project. All departments and personnel will have their share of responsibilities of work in the project and work assignment. All will get their shares of the required amounts of resources needed to get the job done.

All provisions and work efforts/results will have to be 'traded', distributed, and shared by all the departments and personnel in the organization. To enable this, there must be a strong infrastructure in the organization. The infrastructure of an organization is the ability to have all the members in the organization take responsibility in maintaining and managing the organization together, not for one person or a few managing the operation and having all serving this person(s). To have all resources obtained to be shared and traded properly in the organization, all must know what the organization is about and what it is to do and what it can't do. All members and their departments are not to slave away to the person(s) in charge and wait for the person(s) to 'command' any and all decisions. If members and departments are serving the leader(s) and not the organization, proper trading will have ended with little or no infrastructure in the organization.

Power implies provision to area to do work. Trading of collected provisions create the impulse that will enable work to be done. Limited trading lowers the impulse leading little to no work being done. Amongst the provisions being distributed and traded in the infrastructure, the most important is support from the leader.

Stage 2:   ***Trading the existing provisions present in the organization is diminishing or is suspended.***

Deficiency in Communication and Infrastructure

The strength of an organization is the quality of its infrastructure. The infrastructure of the organization is its team. To keep this team and organization together all must be linked together by communication.

A power line linking all the departments together by sharing obtained resources for provision is constructed. To keep all the departments working together and sharing/trading the provisions and work efforts properly will be through communication. All must know what they're doing, how they're going to do it, why they're going to do it, and with what provisions and fellow support they have to do it with. Communication will strengthen the infrastructure, enable the organization to obtain the resources needed, and distribute the job done by the organization.

If there is no communication between the organization and the outsiders of the organization, there will be limits to the lack of resource provisions to be obtained; and lack of means to distribute the work done by the organization. If there is lack of communication in the organization, there is no infrastructure or organization; there is no joint effort to maintain the organization. The people will follow the leader (the organizational charter). If contact and support from the leader drifts away, the effort and enthusiasm (effort to fulfill the goal) of the organization will dissipate.

Stage 3:   ***Lack of communication will result in lack of infrastructure and team work to enable the existence of an organization. Without communication, there will be no provisions to operate the organization.***

SOCIAL MATRIX

A folder lies on the research table. It is a report about an autonomous body held together and operating together by a matrix; a matrix it has formed. This report is of an organization; autonomy of a social body. We will dissect this matrix body. It is simple. It is a chain of command forming a pyramid with a leader at the top point on the pyramid. Above the leader is the charter presenting the ideals of the organization and how it shall present itself by the way it operates. Below the leader are the executives. Each executive is in charge of a department. Each department has its individual post(s) or individual operation(s). Like the mechanical matrix and the bio-matrix, the social matrix (the organization) will gather resources from the external. The raw resources will be produced into provisions for the organization to use and operate with. Leader of the organization, like the server tower in the intranet, and the conscious intelligence that administrates the body through the CNS, will direct the organization through its operations. The leader will deal with the overall of the organization and how it adapts to the world, but not meddle in the internal affairs of the organization. The internal affairs will be left to the executives, the 'lieutenants' to deal with. The 'lieutenants' will not meddle in the individual operations. This will be left to the individual staff member or the project team.

Resources in monetary support, social support, supplies, etc. will be required, provisions required. The social matrix, the organization, will build with the provisions. A social organization is not physical, it's virtuous. Funds from monetary support provide means for credit exchange. Physical supplies, payments and project properties will be obtained by credit exchange. To enable the organization and its projects to carry out, social support and acceptance will be needed. The provisions will be processed to the level they can be exchanged internally amongst the departments and the stations to be used. Information will be gathered from external resources; and produced from the internal departments and operations.

All department and project stations will work coherently with each other sharing funds, supplies, supports, and information with each other. However the organization exists and performs in the real world, the matrix of departments and stations will adapt and make it happen.

The mechanical matrix will work along the communication back bone that exchanges processed sources and the messages for coherent operation. The bio-matrix will work along the communication back bone of the nervous system. Like the mechanical matrix, the power line (the blood vessels) will exchange the sources to be shared by participants in the matrix. The exchange of information, messages and processed sources to be shared internally will be carried out through communication. Communication will be done by social relations, land-line communication, satellite communication and on-line communication. Communication is the back bone of the matrix.

There will be a standardized rule on how the communication exchange will be carried out. To keep the communication alive, all members of the matrix must use it. Messages and information will be exchanged. The leader keeps the organization together through the communication matrix. The leader (CEO, ambassador, Chancellor, president, etc.) and the body of the organization must abide by the plan of operation this organization is formed and operates by. The plan of operation and idea of an organization and goal starts as a thought in the mind; starts out as a plan of action. To turn this plan of action into a plan of operation, all participants in this action will discuss with each other about the rule and idea they are working by. Agreeing to the standard idea and plan of operation, all members of the social matrix will discuss it together officially to develop it and keep the idea alive. Each individual has its own duties and plan of action to carry out its duties. Each plan of action will be constructed in accordance to the organization's plan of operation and the ideal it holds to. The most important factor in a plan of operation is provision to enable the plan of operation to be carried out. No matter how well planned the operation of the organization is, if there is no provision in support, trade credits, supplies and reinforced staff, nothing can be done.

A republic is an organization being maintained by the few chosen for the duty to represent the many. Federal is an organization under a central control. An organization is a structure consisting of an infrastructure of many areas, departments, or stations. The central control of an efficiently run organization is the central control of the infrastructure by a system not by a party of individual(s). It is a system that all in the organization abides by.

<u>Flow Chart of an Organization</u>

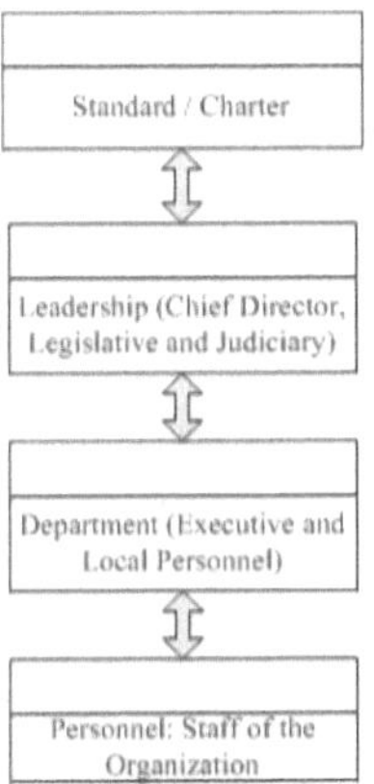

Fig 12[21]

> ***Standard:***   ***The central control of the federation in the organization.***

---

[21] An organization is founded and operates by a charter it is founded by; it is the plan of operation that must be kept 'alive'.

The leadership of the organization (the Chief Executive and the executives of the departments) will manage and guide the organization by the operational plan set in the charter. The leadership is the executor of the organization and its charter by the rules of the charter.

The leadership will keep in contact and aware of the departments and the whole organization. Meetings between the leadership and the executives will be held consistently to keep up with the situation and develop new ways to improve operation according to the charter; and develop better ways in presenting the charter.

The executive of a department will relay all information from the leadership and from other departments of the organization to the department personnel.

> **Leadership:** **Chief Director, Legislative, and Judiciary;**
> **Legislative:** **Board of Directors to authorize what the Chief Director can do or cannot do;**
> **Judiciary:** **Explains the rules of the Charter & Standard of the organization to the Chief Director, to the Legislative, to the departments and to the staff;**
> **Department:** **Each department is headed by its executive who has direct contact with the leadership (the chief director); the executive is the bridge between the leadership and the local personnel;**
> **Staff:** **Is the personnel of the organization.**

All areas in the infrastructure of the organization are important to the structure of the organization. Allowances of trade credits for resources and provisions are provided to each point for the tasks to be done. The allowances are for what is needed and also for the reward for the effort given. From the allowance given, the trade and distribution of the resources (by trade credits) must continue circulating. Each party must give back to the trade by direct trade obtaining products (items or services). Along with direct trade, each party must also give back to the infrastructure where assistance will be needed to keep the structure operating efficiently. This party will give indirect assistance through the system, directive, of the infrastructure. This party can also give direct assistance.

CURRICULAR PLAN OF ACTION: RULES OF ENGAGEMENT

A party must be aware of who is confronting and what he is confronting. He must be fully aware of the advantages and disadvantages he has over the opponent and the situation; and what advantages and disadvantages the opponent and the situation has over him. The main objective is to be fully clear about what the problem is, the best way he solve the problem efficiently, and solve the problem as fast as possible.

If the confrontation and conflict is going to be long, it will be a waste of time, effort and resources. The best way to solve the problem is to handle it as a whole and efficiently. Knowing what the problem is, the source of the problem, one will know how not to break it up into pieces and cause many other problems.

There must be a general plan on what a party is and how this party will identify his problem, his opponent, and how he will confront the problem with the opponent. The general plan of operation is an overall view on what to look for. With establishing the general plan of operation, the central control of the party will have to let each sub-area, sub-party, construct the tactical plan of action to deal with the situation at the local area and situation. The local area will construct an immediate plan of action in accordance to the gathered variables at the local region, and the standard intensions of the general plan of operation of the organization (the party as a whole).

Engineer's Log: Lt. Cmd. Mat: 22201110

"We spent one month in Quadrant A and have spent about one month in Quadrant B. At Quadrant A, our concentration was concentrating in knowing what our potentials are and the potentials of UFS Jonathan. The main concentration is in the physical body of the Jonathan and the physical capacity of each crewmember. We were not to get involved in the local civilizations and local environments. At Quadrant B, we are to develop our skills in operating our vessel and our engineering capacity as we travel with the quantum engineer field. Each crewmember is expected to develop further understanding on how to adapt to the local environment that will different at every location we reach to."

"The primary goal of the UFS Jonathan and its crew is to learn about the regions beyond Earth's local star system; and also learn how to develop the capacity of the ship (the vessel and the crew) without interfering with the locals. The primary infrastructure of the UFS Jonathan is keeping autonomy on the vessel amongst the crew. Each person must learn how to relate with each other and respect each other before we can begin making judgment on how we shall relate with the locals."

"The engine has its faults leaving difficulty(s) with local stations and areas. The power packets were faulty. Knowing what the defects were in the power packets, we were able to know what the source of the problem may be. The problem was with the power packets. The source for the production of the power supply was fine. It must be the power production or the production of the power packets that may be faulty."

"In Sun Tzu's philosophy, one must know himself and know his opponent before he can attempt to confront his opponent. If one does not know himself, his opponent, or the situation, he will have a lack of advantage for victory."

Doctor's Log: Cmd. Carl: 22201110

"Once entering into Quadrant B and having our stay here, each member of the crew has developed his/her plan on how to adapt to the situation. Those with birth-defect(s) and those who have developed injury during this journey have established means in dealing with their medical situations to handle their problems. Knowing the physical structures of their bodies and the situations they will be encountering, they develop confidence in carrying out their duties at their posts."

"The defect in several crew members was power packets (blood cells). Two were found to have blood deficiency(s) leading to bleeding problems. One had cancer in his blood."

Counselor's Log: Lt. Cmd. Simmons: 22201110

"Some crew members had difficulties at their posts trying to work there or trying to get the job done. Some had difficulties with their health. These problems brought about psychological difficulties. They had to learn how to adapt to their situations and not let their affairs disrupt their duty(s). Their advantages are knowing what their problems are and knowing potentials and limits are."

Captain's Log: Captain Jameson: 22201110

"So far, we have concentrated on how to develop our bodies, and the surface structure of the vessel to adapt to the situations we are and will be encountering. We have avoided confrontation with civilizations. As Sun Tzu advised that it will not be wise to confront if there is no preparation and expectation of victory. In his advice, there is victory if the reward is not accelerating and cannot be used to bring further rewards in the future. Advantage of knowing self and knowing opponent brings rewarding victory."

"The construction of the vessel had started as was designed. With time, construction of the vessel required adjustment to the design due to situations. With the adjustment to the frame of the vessel, construction of the crew's organization and operation had to be mapped during the vessel's construction at the Alpha Station. With time, there will be expectance of further changes (adjustments) to be made during the ventures of the Jonathan and her crew."

"Mapping out the design of the vessel and the organization of the crew can be recognized as simulating the DNA of the body of a Homo Sapient Erectus. With time, the infrastructure and structure of the vessel will change; the infrastructure and the operational structure of the crew will also change. The network of operations of all the stations and the areas in the vessel is the infrastructure of the vessel. The operation of the entire autonomous network of the vessel as a whole is the vessel's structure. The operational performance of each crew member at each station and each area form the infrastructure of the crew. The autonomous network of the crew members forms the autonomy, and structure, of the crew and operations. With time, the infrastructure and the structure of the ship, the vessel and its crew, will adapt to the situations experienced and learned."

"A young child learns to stand, walk and develop his body to relate to the environment around him. As a child learns and adapts, so too must a ship when she is born (commissioned) and leaves port. The venture into Quadrant A was like the beginning experiences of a young child. At Quadrant B, this young child (the UFS Jonathan) uses what he has learned and develops it."

DIPLOMATIC BUSINESS OPERATION

To avoid further opponents and many other opponents, do not be aggressive toward them. Know what the problem is so the opposing parties will join together to solve the problem together; opposing parties will become allies together. Members of the autonomous matrix are allies; they will share their resources (information and supplies). To maintain the network, communication must be established and maintained. The communication network will ensure the infrastructure of the structural body of the organization, the ship, and the animal body.

The basis for the momentum in the network is by memory. Memory provides gathered data and work data and work memory for further work to be done. Work memory will enable communication to maintain autonomy and alliance. Formulated memory file will capture incoming data. The data will not be lost as the work memory uses the data constantly and new work file(s) and data to be used.

Communications Officer's Log: Lt. Cmd. James: 22201110

"Communication concentrates on passing messages from station to station, from bridge to ship, for what is needed and what is to be done. The operational procedure and action of each station is planned out in accordance to the primary operational plan of the ship (crew and vessel) and the variable(s) of the situation at the location of the station. The immediate operational procedure at the station is the local station's plan of action. As the immediate plan of action is worked upon with the incoming data, this worked upon plan of action becomes incoming data also. The formulation of the immediate plans of actions, formulating adjustments in the ship's plan of operation, captures the incoming data to be remembered and worked with. If there is no present formulation to use and work with the data, the incoming data will drift around looking for a storage area. If the data is not used, it will be lost. This is surface work memory, and long stored archive memory."

"Formulated files must be present giving purpose for the data. The formulation and the incoming data becomes a message to be shared with specific transmission target(s) (station(s) and the bridge)."

"The surface structure of the vessel and the infrastructure of the stations have changed somewhat since we ventured off from the Alpha Station. Messages have to be sent from station to station on how to have the stations work coherently together. Messages will be sent to the bridge and the CNC of the vessel for the bridge officers and the ships computer to manage and operate the ship."

"The CNC is the primary processor and central control of the entire ship computer. The infrastructure of the station consoles forms the whole ship computer. The ship computer is the vessel. The infrastructure of crew member(s) forms the structure of the crew and how the crew operates."

"The infrastructure of different stations will work coherently with each other so the structural operation of the ship will adapt to the situation. The ship's computer extends externally. The probes sent out to gather data to form virtual impression of the external object enable the ship computer, the ship to see externally. The ship will learn how to adapt to the external environment physically and socially."

Doctor's Log: Cmd. Carl: 22201110

"As the CNC of the ship control communication and operation of the ship's infrastructure, the brain stem of the animal body controls the organs and the nervous system within the animal body. As time passes, each organ grows and develops manipulating the growth and development of the entire body. The organs and cellular areas communicate with each other through neurons in the nervous system, and blood cells in the blood vessels (arteries and veins)."

"Crew member with Factor VII Deficiency has difficulty in healing/sealing his wound when the body or organ is breached. The blood cells are not bringing the sufficient amount of proteins or nutrients to help the area regenerate the cells and tissues of the area. Communication through nervous system to all organs and all areas in this body to work coherently on the breaching of the skins, manipulate other parts of the body to assist in the blocking of the breached area."

"Crew member with cancerous blood cells have faulty blood cells that are regenerating faster than clean healthy blood cells are. The massively growing body of faulty blood cells is causing damage to the body's organs and cellular areas. Healthy cells bonding with healthy cells regenerate healthy cells. Faulty cells bonding with faulty cells or healthy cells regenerate faulty cells. This crew member will have to monitor his body through his nervous system. He will learn to adapt to difficulties as he works at his station and find means to compensate for loss of time. His fellow crew members will have to work with him as a team and find means to get the job(s) done in time."

"Crew member with Factor VIII Deficiency has difficulty stopping or slowing down the blood flow through the wound when the body surface is breached. Messages through the nervous system and blood vessels can only try to avoid the body from getting surface wounds. Messages through the nervous system are direct and clear. The blood cells only encourage reflexive reaction when movement and momentum occurs."

"Crew member with visual problem can take notice by sighting, but cannot focus in what is seen. The attempt to focus strains the entire body. The CNS and brain stem must direct message from the brain to the optical nerves to stop focusing and suspend visual operations. The nervous system will have to direct message(s) to specific organs and areas to work coherently together. The infrastructure will have the body adapting to the situation."

"Crew member with difficulty(s) with his nervous system (seizure disorder) have to be trained to avoid sudden suspension of his body from operation at the post. Before the self-awareness and consciousness of the person is suspended, the person must instruct the brain stem and the nervous system to operate without control from the brain (the self-aware conscious intelligence). The organs and mobile areas will be trained to receive simple instructions on what to do. The pre-planned operation will have the area do as planned and directly manipulate other areas to react by reflexive reaction."

"All areas in the body are pre-planned for immediate action to receive data and construct instructions and data according to the ultimate plan of operation."

Counselor's Log: Lt. Cmd. Simmons: 22201110

"As all areas within the infrastructure of the ship communicate with each other, and the all areas within the infrastructure of the animal body communicate with each other, so must the infrastructure of the alliance. All must respect each other and work with each other. Each area may compete with each other to enable the best way to handle the problem, but the areas must not combat with each other. Allies will share notes and opinions on how to confront the problem, but they must not waste time, effort and resources to combat with each other."

Captain's Log: Captain Jameson: 22201110

"The primary factor in an infrastructure is communication. Messages and data sent and received must have a formulated memory space to stay or they will be lost and forgotten. The plan of action of the local area will be prepared to receive incoming data. The constructed plan of action for the local area becomes the incoming data for the primary plan of operation for the whole structure. The reconstructed plan of operation becomes a factor in the plan of action of the local area and local station."

"The infrastructure of different plans of actions will work together to form the structure of the body of the ship (vessel and crew). Specific station(s) and specific area(s) will be working with each other for the specific purpose of adapting to a situation. They form an infrastructure (cloud) of their own. Clouds will work with other clouds forming an infrastructure of clouds. The infrastructure of clouds the autonomous structure of the vessel (a carrier body that is delivering a crew, a staff, or an idea)."

INCORPORATED STRUCTURE

A whole party consists of many sub-parties. The sub-parties will work together autonomously. This autonomy is held together by a power (resource) sharing network, and a communication network. There will be no prejudice, personal bias, of superiority or inferiority toward each other. The sub-parties, posts, will recognize each other and respect other's rank, position and duty. Each post in the matrix will be assigned to his position with discretion of skills and qualifications as required for the work to be done. There will be a respect of senior and junior for the task and responsibility. Respect of rank, position and duty does not give reason for personal bias.

The pyramid flow chart of a republic is formulated by rank, position and duty through skills and qualifications as required in maintaining order. Personal prejudice will cause internal conflict within the whole party and organization. The bias sub-parties will become opponents to each other in the internal conflict. This is the infrastructure of the body formulating the structural body. Work memory and storage of data by usage of the data will enable communication and distribution of resources in maintaining the structure. In the autonomy, all parties (all allies) are equal to each other no matter the discretion in rank, position and duty. Each post and area has its purpose incorporating fellow posts and their work together. Each post will support fellow posts in the network and maintain the autonomy together with fellow posts. The structural body is sovereignty as a whole. It is not a dictatorship; a sovereignty over sovereignty(s) over sovereignty(s) cont.

Engineer's Log: Cmd. Mat: 22201110

> "The ship, and the ship computer, is broken down into different areas of operation and different locations in the operations. Different areas, and locations, are broken down to station(s). The area is not superior to the station; it's only

higher in responsibility and duty to the station. The area is responsible in monitoring more than one station working together. Areas work in accordance to the department(s) that is controlled/monitored by ship computer's primary processor (the CNC)."

"Stations in the area will work together and share information with each other to get the job done by the area. One station will be responsible in monitoring the messages and operations of the area and the stations. Without a station to monitor the area, the stations in the area will be operating chaotically without order. If station(s) are not doing its share in the job assigned to the area, the area will fail and the job will not be successfully completed."

"The station monitoring all the areas and their stations will ensure all stations and all areas are working together in accordance to the department's responsibility(s)."

"The CNC station will monitor the entire operation of the ship by managing the cooperation and coherency of all the stations in the ship computer (the ship)."

"Each station console is subconsciously aware with the preprogramming to receive data and apply them to the station's operation. At each station console, there will be a crew member that will provide the conscious self-awareness to reason why or why not the station shall do something."

Communications Officer's Log: Lt. Cmd. James: 22201110

"The communication network in the ship computer enables the stations on board the ship to communicate with each other and work with each other. The preprogramming(s) in each station console provides work file(s) to capture the incoming data and construct operational procedures (immediate plan of action) and possibly new work file(s) (new general plan of action or immediate plan of operation for that station). An immediate plan of action or a general plan of action for the station will be constructed."

Doctor's Log: Cmd. Carl: 22201110

"The DNA maps the vessel body of the Homo Sapient Erectus as the nautical design maps out the vessel body of a ship. The DNA, the map, of the body sets out the primary (general) operational plan for the body. The plan of operation sets out the basis for the general plan of action for the cellular station and motor area at the location of the body. The varying data and information that affects the location of the body will determine how that location's cellular stations and cellular area will act upon the situation. Whatever plan of action the station and area will do, tissues will be constructed to enable momentum and response."

"The cells will receive the type and amount of power and supplies the cell will need for reproduction (regeneration) of cells and tissues for momentum and response. The cellular stations (the cells) in the motor area will work together to maintain and operate the motor area. The different motor areas (organs) at different locations around the body will work coherently together to maintain the autonomy (anatomy) of the body. Whatever the body must do to adapt to the situation, cells and areas at different locations in the body will do whatever possible with the incoming data from the external environment and internal environment (the condition the body is in) to adapt. If the cell(s) at the location cannot respond properly, the entire body will have to have all areas in the body work coherently together to adapt and provide the proper response."

"There is no superiority inferiority complex amongst the cells in the body. All cellular stations have their purpose at their locations. The cellular stations are at their higher or lower duty position only. If there is no coherency, the body will deteriorate. All cellular stations and cellular areas must regenerate fast producing healthy cells to adapt and compensate for any losses. If the healthy cells are not strong enough regenerate fast enough, cancer will have occurred. The cells carrying the power and supplies (blood cells) to the surface cells are damaged and carrying insufficient power and supplies for regeneration, damage and caner will spread being brought by the blood cells."

"Neuron cells carry charges through the nervous network. Like bytes delivering messages through charges and signals, neuron cells will deliver messages by signals to cellular stations and cellular areas to perform (move and respond). Each cellular station and each cellular motor area have been preprogrammed to move and respond according to a signal. All it needs is the type of signal to set off momentum and response. The momentum and response of one station or area will set off other stations and areas by reflexive reaction without the brain stem (the CNC of the ship) to send signals to other stations and areas. With seizure disorder, the internal environment set off a neuron signal to station(s) and area(s) to act. The other station(s) and area(s) will respond reflexively without signal from the CNS (the brain stem, and CNC of the computer). The person will have to intelligently train his brain stem and body to respond subconsciously to avoid any problem(s) should seizure occur."

Counselor's Log: Lt. Cmd. Simmons: 22201110

"All crew members, no matter how different their ranks, positions, and duties, respect each other and work together with no aggressions toward each other. It is the rank, position and duty that is higher or lower, not the person. Each crew member will respect each other as persons of same qualities, and will respect each other's rank and position while at duty at station and location. They will respect each other's rank, and also each other's personal character (race, color, gender, age, class, and ethnicity)."

"Each individual will work at their post with experience and knowledge. Working at his post long enough, and on board the vessel long enough, the individual will have a clear understanding if the ship's plan of operation and his personal plan of action. With understanding of the plans, he will know how to store and remember the data from the external archive and the various situations that is presented. He will keep the memory and data alive by using them and sharing them with others."

"With sharing information and messages, they will share supplies. At their posts and positions, they will know what they will need and how much. Some will need more and some will need less according to the situation and what is to be done. No matter how much the post will need, the individual will know not to hoard over the power and supplies. Each post and station must work coherently with each other to maintain the ship (the vessel and the crew). Without coherency, there is no autonomy. Without autonomy, there will be no ship. All must work together; all must make sacrifices together."

DISCREPANCY IN THE OPERATION

Social mechanics simulates bio mechanics and non-bio mechanics. To maintain the mechanical structure, conflict(s) within the structure must be overcome. The alliance of the different parties will work together to form the autonomy and internal structure of the organization. The internal structure of the organization is by the general plan of the organization. Each sub-party in the autonomy will be responsible for its immediate/local plan of action. The local plan of action of each sub-area will work with each other and support each other in their mass autonomy.

Each structural body has an ultimate plan of operation holding the entire body together on its purpose of existence and operation. Each location and post in the autonomous body has its immediate plan of action for immediate action. Each plan of action will be formulated in accordance with the structural body's plan of operation and the immediate variable(s) at the situation and location.

Captain's Log: Captain Jameson: 22201110

> "Engineering and Communications explained clearly how the vessel and her crew will work together to maintain the autonomy of the ship. The Doctor gave a clear simulation of the animal body with the vessel. The Counselor explained clearly about the mentality of the crew members and how they will perform together. The infrastructure of the ship (the vessel and the crew) constructs the structure of the ship. The ship would be the organization/community in society. The vessel is the establishment and carrier of an idea to be represented by the staff. The crew is the staff. Whether we are operating a nautical ship or a social

organization, the procedure in operating is as the seniors have presented their opinions on it."

"The start of our venture was not easy. It was a test of our social autonomy and the physical structure of the vessel. The medial review showed how individuals had their difficulties and how they must adapt to their situations. The rest of the crew will have to work along to keep the ship in functional order. The main thing crew members must remember is that they must respect each other's personal character and situation and never bring attention to them. High and low by rank, position and duty do reason for personal thoughts and bias; no personal bias will be accepted."

"The ship's structure (vessel structure and operational structure of the crew) must be adjusted to adapt to the environment. The surface structure of the vessel will need to be changed to adapt to the power and condition regarding to the quantum field and tunnel. The stations and areas in the hull of the vessel will have to make adjustments; so too must the power lines and the communication lines. The positioning of the posts will have to be adjusted; so too must the operational procedures of the different post (the different stations and the different areas)."

"As we learn how to maintain the autonomy of the ship, we will learn how to relate with the environments and communities in the different quadrants we will be entering into. Our relations with the civilizations must be diplomatic and we must not interfere with them. If the civilization's technology and knowledge are not similar to our level of technology and knowledge, we must not introduce ourselves or we will be interfering with their development. We must avoid forming a dominion. We are not here to dominate their society. We are only here to learn about them."

"Resources, power and supplies, are produced by area(s) and distributed all over the body to be shared by the all areas and all stations in the body. In a social body, an organization or business body, distribution of resources will be done by exchange of trade credits. Resources will be valued in trade credits. Trade credits will be awarded to station posts for the amount of resources it will require to do its job. Trade credits will be awarded to crew/staff member for the effort individual's performance. The station will reward the body for trade credits by performing its task(s) efficiently. The staff member will reward the body for the credits by keeping the trade flow active at all times allowing all other areas to have a share in the trade market of the resources through the trade credits."

"The value in the resources, the station or the staff member is not in the amount of trade credit that it is obtained by but how well it performs."

VENTURE AHEAD

THE VENTURE CARRIES ON

It has been months since the Jonathan (the vessel and the crew) has left port and have begun restructuring itself. The surface structure had to adapt to the physical environments of different star systems. As the surface structure is being developed, the infrastructure (the stations and areas) had to be reorganized or constructed.

The crew of the Jonathan is large and will be venturing through deep space for a long time. We have to learn to relate with each other as a family. No matter how different each individual's personal history may be, family members will learn to accept each other's differences to work with each other and live with each other. We will learn more about the physiology of the Homo Sapient Erectus, the human anatomy. As we learn how the human body develops and recover by regeneration; we will learn how the stations and areas in the hull of the Jonathan can operate with productive results.

Our experiences in the Academy and prior field training ventures have prepared us in how to operate the machineries on board the Jonathan. Our further experiences will prepare us to develop our understanding of deep space. Through experience, we formulate preparation(s) to receive data and remember them. Data from information gathered will be used with previously formulated plans to construct new plans. Plans will be refined and remembered. Data will be remembered as they are being used and worked upon.

Knowing the formulated general plan of action, the crewmember will know how to formulate the immediate plan of action with the data provided. The crewmember will remember the data and the situation by knowing what to do. The ship (the vessel and the crew) will either know or not know and keep the data and plan in consistent usage.

Structural Condition / Infrastructure

Crewmember 7183888003 has been with the ship since it left Alpha Station. He has been very close with the crew and knows them more than the Staff Officer does. Crewmember 7183888003 has been assigned by the UF Fleet Command to get a full evaluation of the vessel's operation and the crew's personal and professional performance. As the Jonathan approaches the Alpha Station, 7183888003 prepares an entire report for the Fleet Command. To be clear, he chooses to personalize the report. He has chosen to relate the ship's performance in deep space with 7 individuals' personal affairs.

DNA creates a general map of the body, not the person. Like any architectural design, the structure will have to build in accordance to the general design and the unexpected situation. Crewmember 1966060434 was in fine condition during birth. He was developing excellently in his early childhood. When he entered into the Academy, he was given an excellent report on his physical health and mental health. His bones and body frame were in excellent condition. Crewmember 1966060434 was a student of vessel architecture and structural formation. He has had experience in several voyages on several vessels to learn how the vessel structure will perform under the condition of empty space. On the Jonathan, crewmember 1966060434 was assigned to the Engineering Department to observe and give review of the structural performance of the vessel. He will be travelling from station to station, from area to area, to review the consoles, the power lines, and the communication lines. He was assigned under Lt. Cmd. Mat.

There was no problem when leaving the Alpha Station and entering the quantum tunnel. Sudden turbulence caused pressure on the surface of the hull. Crewmember 1966060434 went around the stations and areas to make reviews of the situation. Crewmember 1966060434 found that the material used to construct the infrastructural surface, and the structural surface of the hull, was not as strong as thought to be. The testing of the material in a controlled environment that did not involve quantum barrier and quantum tunnel showed the material as excellent and strong. Once the quantum tunnel and then encountering a massive turbulence, the material was not as strong as thought to be.

To compensate, the quantum energy used by the vessel will have to be directed to the formation of the material used in the infrastructure to strengthen the material and the structural surface. The procedure(s) in travelling through the tunnel and travelling by impulse power had to be reformulated. The surface design of the vessel hull had to be adjusted to enable safe motion during the travel. With the change of the external surface, the architecture of the infrastructure had to be changed. Crewmember 1966060434 worked with Lt. Cmd. Mat to redesign and adjust the infrastructure; the repositioning of the stations and areas. New locations had to be reconstructed.

During the turbulence, crewmember 1966060434 had difficulties with the frame structure of his body, his bones. He felt great pain. It has been found that deep space had affected his bone structure. Gravitational field and controlled environment during brief space travels showed no effect on the bone structure. Nobody has tested bones in quantum field or deep space (long period in space).

As he took his tour of the vessel, crewmember 1966060434 began to feel great pain. He noticed that the pain was not from his flesh but was deeper, during movement. It appeared that the pain from his bones and joints. He began to slouch and could barely stand up straight. Lt. Cmd. Mat instructed crewmember 1966060434 to go to the infirmary. At the infirmary, Doctor Carl found that the bones had weakened. Records have shown that the bones were strong before the journey on the Jonathan. After a period of time in the quantum tunnel and deep space, the bones were weakened. The turbulence and the constant movement brought difficulty and pain. Doctor Carl prescribed a treatment. The treatment involves medication, alignment by energy and force, proper diet, and no strenuous work.

During the months in deep space, crewmember 1966060434 will continue his duty patrolling the vessel and report of any situation with the vessel hull. He is to be working with an assistant and mentor this crewmember who will reach toward areas that are only reachable by strenuous effort. He enjoyed space walks on the external surface of the hull, but he cannot do that anymore. His apprentice will do that alone now.

As crewmember 1966060434 had to avoid strenuous confrontations, so too must the Jonathan. The formation of the hull and the arrangement of the stations and areas enable the Jonathan to travel far and at great speed; but the Jonathan must avoid close contacts with orbital force, gravitational force, and turbulent force. Jonathan's mission is research and observation. If the civilization has capability of deep space travel and quantum power, Jonathan can make direct contact. The Jonathan can only stay in the outer orbit. The representatives of the civilization will have to meet half way with our representatives in space.

The structure of the vessel hull is by the arrangement of the points in the infrastructure of the vessel. The strength of the surface in the infrastructure is the material used to construct the surface. The strength and structure of the crew is the arrangement and infrastructure of the organization of the crew. Crewmembers will be assigned in accordance to their qualifications and satisfaction. They will form clouds of specific fields to share information on a specific field of operation from different areas. A larger cloud will hold all these clouds of specific fields together and work with each other coherently. All areas will work coherently together under this mass cloud, the ship.

Entering into Quadrant A, the ship found difficulties with its physical structure which caused disruption in the arrangements and calmness in the crew. Before entering into the tunnel to enter into Quadrant B, arrangements had to be made to strengthen the hull and the structural surface of the hull. Arrangement had to be made to strengthen the physical condition of the Jonathan and means to prevent any further physical threats to the physical surface of the vessel.

Before entering into Quadrant B, the arrangement and organization of the crew had to be improved. The crew had to find calmness to travel in deep space together. There must be a trust in trading with each other, working with each other, and helping each other.

There are crewmen traveling in the hull every moment. Their routines are changing every time they come up to a point where improvements are advised. They are in deep space now and must adapt to the change and get comfortable with their new environment. The structure of the crew and its organization is founded in accordance to the infrastructure of organs, departmental work areas. There will be clouds within clouds within clouds…etc. The crewmen within a cloud will communicate with each other sharing information and resources with each other. Crewmen of different clouds will share information and resources with each other in accordance to their tasks and fields. This infrastructure of clouds will share information, resources and crewmen available.

As we travelled on to Quadrants C and D, we learned to strengthen the physical structure of Jonathan's hull and the structure of the organization of the crew. As we approach the Alpha Station, each crewmember were able to write his/her own manual on how to travel on a Jonathan Class vessel, usage of quantum power, co-relations on the ship in deep space, and diplomatic relations with other cultures and civilizations.

Station(s) and area(s) at specific locations will require work to be done to strengthen the structure. The weaker the material, the more effort will be done to strengthen the structure and the infrastructure to adjust and work effort at the location. The more effort required the more power required.

Power Production

Crewmember 7183888003 is not an expert in any field. He is knowledgeable and experienced in all fields and can do anything and will be assigned anywhere. He is a jack of all trades, but he can only do one task at a time. He will not be assigned to another station or another task until his present assignment is completed. As a jack of all trades, crewmember 7183888003 will travel all over the ship knowing all the people at all the stations. He will know all the crewmembers; learn about them and experience their work performances.

The UFS Jonathan is testing a new type of power produced and a new class of vessel that will be using such power type. There are 2 engines. The primary engine is to produce the power, energy source that will be used by the vessel. The 2nd engine will produce the means to deliver the power and supply to the distinct locations. Different locations will use the same power but different supplies to produce their products, supply or service. The supply will be added on to the power packets to be delivered to other locations.

Crewmember 1112789299 is trained and experienced in power production and distribution. He was assigned to engineering; assigned to the 1st engine. He was to monitor what it is producing and how it is performing.

After the wave incident with the wave turbulence in Quadrant A, crewmember 1112789299 was one of the many who were injured resulting in injuries and bleeding. It appeared that 1112789299's injuries were not severe but his bleeding was. Doctor Carl reviewed his condition and found that this crewmember may have blood defect. Looking through this patient's medical records, he found that there were no sign of blood defect or any health problem. Crewmember 1112789299 has Factor 8 Deficiency, Hemophilia. It had appeared that this problem was buried away until something triggers it to take effect on the body.

The density and strength of the blood determining the flow of the blood is Factor 8. It appears that crewmember 1112789299 has low density in his blood so his blood flows out like water once the blood vessel is breached. The type of blood content in any person's blood is hereditary. It is in the mapping of the power lines (the blood lines) and the surface structure of the body. Factor 8 Deficiency is in the DNA mapping of the blood, affecting the mapping of the blood lines and the body structure. To avoid injuries and bleeding, crewmember 1112789299 will have to be careful and avoid damaging encounters. Effects on the body's movement will affect the body's development. The formation of the blood vessels must be coherent with the surface structure of the body.

During the overview of the damages from the turbulence, Engineering found that the power and supplies provided to the stations were not at full capacity. The power was leaking out of the power lines, inside the hull and outside the hull. The fast leakage; was it due to the power produced by the 1st engine or the power packets produced by the 2nd engine. To determine if it's engine 1 or engine 2, we will have to wait until we get back to Alpha Station to do an overhaul of the vessel. As the physician(s) will have to do a full evaluation on the patient which will require surgical entries and complicated tests, the engineer(s) at the port will have to strip the whole vessel apart and check every piece with intricately.

1st Lt. 6606362082 is experienced in structural engineering since the Academy. His experience is structural powering, providing power (delivering power) for use. On the Jonathan, Lt. 6606362082 was assigned to the 2nd engine to monitor the production of power packets for delivery of power and supplies. Part of duty is to take a tour of the vessel and review the performance of the stations and observe how the power and supplies are delivered and used. During his tour of the vessel in Quadrant A, the experience with the wave turbulence occurred. Like many injuries, there was bleeding. Lt. 6606362082's injury was not severely injured and was not bleeding out fast like crewmember 1112789299 was.

At the infirmary, medical technicians noticed this and reported it to Doctor Carl. Doctor Carl reviewed the Lt.'s medical records and his condition. The doctor found that this patient had an excellent medical history since birth. There was nothing noticeable with the simple blood test. They didn't know what else to look for so they didn't look for it. He passed through the Academy and from vessel to vessel with a record of fine medical health. There was never an injury that required the cells to do much work to regenerate and seal the wound.

After some blood tests, Doctor Carl found that 1st Lt. 6606362082 has Factor 7 Deficiency. Factor 7 is content in the blood that provides assistance to the cells to regenerate. When an area of the body is injured, bleeding will occur. The cell(s) of that area will have to start regenerating to seal the wound. The cell(s) will require the necessary type of protein to regenerate. The level of this protein that the blood cell can provide is in Factor 7. With Factor 7 Deficiency, the skin cells will take longer to regenerate because they will have to do work with what is available. But, the damaged area will seal. Lt. 6606362082 can continue his tour of duty and assignments, but carefully. He can participate in strenuous work, but avoid deep cuts and severe wounds.

During his tour in Quadrant A, 1st Lt. 6606362082 experienced cuts several times. They were not deep cuts but the wounds were healing slowly. The bleeding slowly stopped. The bleeding was not severe so he was not weakened. The bleeding did annoy him and his work station. He had to develop new routines and new procedures to cover the wounds and not let the bandages or wounds affect his performance.

By the time he reached Quadrant B, Lt. 6606362082 learned to do physically active work and avoid extensive wounds or cuts. He found ways to cover his wounds and help it seal normally. While in Quadrants C & D, he participated in the 'away missions' several times to observe the power sources of the environments and learn how the civilizations produced power, delivered the power and used it. Because the Jonathan is on a diplomatic mission, the ship and the teams must be inconspicuous. They must not disturb the civilization.

Like 1st Lt. 6606362082, the Jonathan was experiencing problems in its power and operations. The stations are not receiving the amount of power and supplies required for satisfactory operation. It may be the power produced or the power packets. We will not know until we reach Alpha Station and do the overhaul. We will have to develop procedures in using power effectively. Stations may have to ration the resources determining which station and area will need the necessary amount of resources to deal with the immediate situation at the location. All stations will have to make sacrifices and work coherently together.

1st Lt. 1967072720 was recorded as fit and strong at birth, at young childhood and early adulthood. He developed expertise in communications at the Academy and at several vessels. On the Jonathan, Lt. 1967072720 was assigned to the Communications Department and stationed at the bridge. The Lt. is to observe the coherency of the stations and areas by communication and power distribution (exchange of power and supplies). The Lt. will observe and determine the reflexive responses of the stations.

During the tour at Quadrant A, 1st Lt. 1967072720 got severely ill. While at the infirmary, Doctor Carl found that the lieutenant's cells were defective. With further tests, the doctor determined that something may have damaged the blood cells in the lieutenant's body. The cells are to use the resources, the proteins and nutrients, delivered from the blood cells to regenerate and continue operation. It appears the blood cells are defective and delivering poor amounts of, or poor quantity, or proteins and nutrients to the cells of the organs. The organs regenerate and imitate the quality of what they are given. If it's by healthy blood cells, the organs will regenerate healthy cells. As defective cells grow and dominate the organ and area, caner has occurred.

Blood cells regenerate from the protein and nutrient they carry to carry them onward. Defective blood cells will deliver defective supplies causing defective organ cells. Regeneration of defective blood cells is Leukemia. 1st Lt. 1967072720 has Leukemia. The Jonathan was 'ill'. Its power packets and resources may be defective. The stations were not operating effectively. The Jonathan must find ways to use what they can gather. The stations, areas and power lines had to be realigned so the new ration of resources can be used effectively. While in Quadrants C & D, the Jonathan developed new ways in rationing; and developed new structural designs for the infrastructure and the structure to use the rations effectively.

The Jonathan may have defective power packets that are bringing poor resources to the stations and areas. The poor resources are causing the resources to leak out very fast when the power line is breached; and do not provide the necessary amount of resources to the stations and areas to operate efficiently. The vessel structure will have to be refined to enable the stations and areas to operate with the resources they are provided with giving satisfactory or excellent results. Routines will have to be rearranged so rationing will be effective.

Given resources will be by allowance. Each station and each area will be given allowances for their operations. Rationing will be in accordance to the situation and the needs to maintain coherency. On board the Jonathan, the stations will be given their allowances, and the crewmembers will be given their allowances. The allowances for the resources to be received will be used by direct transfer of product produced with specific station(s) and direct transfer of some resources back to the power line where the resources have come from. The allowances are by trade credits for power and supplies.

Allowances will be exchanged for personal needs, and also to sustain the entire system (the infrastructure of the vessel). There will be stations that must be kept operational and will be needed at all times; and there will be stations that are not needed at all times but must be kept operational at all times to be ready when needed. Allowances will be given in accordance to the needs at the moment.

Rationing of allowances was created for deep space travel and the condition the vessel is in. Procedures in rationing have been formulated for the new manual to be used by the Academy.

If there is any hoarding, there will be a clot of power and supply in an area in the network. In an autonomous machine like the vessel hull of the Jonathan, clotting will be causing a buildup of power and supply in one area causing a lack of power and supply to other areas. In a biological body, this will cause a cramp. The crewmember with seizure disorder had seizures that resulted in convulsions.

Power production and power distribution are the same in the autonomic structure of a machine, a biological body of an animal, and the infrastructure of the trade market in a civilization or organization. The flow chart of a republic gives a clear impression of this structure.

The power will be delivered to the station and area to do work; to strengthen (reproduce or regenerate) operation at the location. Power will be required to do the work of delivering the necessary amount of power to location to do work. The weaker the power being delivered, or the weaker the means in deliver the power to do work, the more power required to be delivered to location to do necessary work.

All stations must stay active to keep the newly produced resources (power and supplies) used and circulated to replenish the resources needed for work to be done. If supply of newly produced resources is weak, work will exhaust the power and supplies in the stations all over exhausting the vessel body.

Network Control

Crewmember 7183888003 is a jack of all trades and is experienced in all fields. While in Quadrant B, he is assigned to communications. He is to work with crewmember 1966060445 at a communications post to observe and gather data from space. While crewmember 1966060445 boarded the Jonathan, he had to wear lenses. His eyes were already having difficulties; but the difficulties were not severe. He has been at this post for a while and sitting at the console monitor visual sightings. With time, his eyes got worse. He could barely see any more. He could take sighting of an object, but he cannot get a clear focus of whom or what is there.

The human body has 5 known physical senses. He learns through them. There is a snake that could not see clearly. It could not see what is there, but it can detect the object by the infrared. It has a very sensitive olfactory sensory that can detect an object distant away by the smell of it. It can identify the object by the taste of it. Its somatic sensory can detect the movement of the object and its distance by the feeling the disturbance in the air, environment.

The bat is blind, has no visual perspective of its surroundings. Its audio sensory is so sensitive that it can detect any disturbance in the air by sound and approach toward that sound. Its somatic sensory is so sensitive that its body and wings can make immediate adjustments in flight to adapt to the environment and stay in the air to approach toward the target instantly without instruction from the brain.

Crewmember 1966060445 is just near blind but he can move around as if he could see. He touches his console and flows through the console board faster than any person who can see. He could walk around the area as if he could see. Crewmember 7183888003 could see but he stalls on the console board trying to think and decide which key to press. While walking around the station area, stumbles on his legs and near the console stands. Crewmember 7183888003 had more difficulties in the station area than crewmember 1966060445 did.

One day, crewmember 7183888003 joined crewmember 1966060445 in 1966060445's appointment at the infirmary. Crewmember 1966060445 is to have his regular medical review. After the regular medical review, 1966060445 gave Doctor Carl permission to know about his medial situation and explain to him of his situation. The doctor explained to crewmember 7183888003 that the five physical senses (audio, visual, gustatory, olfactory, and somatic) work coherently together to help the body and mind learn and help the body move with ease.

In crewmember 1966060445's present situation with little vision, he has prevented his eyes from trying to make visual contact and strengthen his other senses to make clear impressions of the presence. Different areas will have different sensory capacities. The different areas with different capacity will remember experiences differently and develop plans to deal with the similar situations again. Part of the plan is to work coherently with other areas. It is the body and its cellular stations that will remember and operate on their own, not the brain. If crewmember 1966060445 chooses to understand and remember what his body is doing, 1966060445 will store the memory in the archive of the long term memory. He must not disturb the surface work memory at his brain with minor details that can be dealt with by the cellular stations all around his body.

It is his body that remembers how to walk through the work area with ease without having to deceive the brain having the brain decide whether he should or should not do something. At console, crewmember 1966060445 will give a simple charge of instruction from the brain. The body will do the rest by general memory plan that has been set up.

The Jonathan has a poor visual capacity. It has difficulty visualizing at a distance. Audio and somatic can detect disturbance in space. Probes and energy will be sent out to identify the presence. If the presence shows strong force, the Jonathan will try to avoid it. After all encounters the Jonathan has faced since leaving the Alpha Station, each station and area has remembered the general plans of action and immediate plans of action constructed to deal with situations. Each station and each area knows what to do without having to disturb the bridge and the seniors. The vessel can travel through space without disturbing the crew.

Crewmember 7183888003 has just been assigned to the bridge communications post and assist Ensign 1966060412. They are to monitor the overall detections inside the hull and outside of the hull of the Jonathan. When Ensign 1966060412 entered into the Academy, he was in fine health and showed no problem with his physical reflexes or his physical sensory. He showed no medical problems when he boarded the Jonathan. During the turbulence in Quadrant A, was struck in the head. He was struck on the rear of the left side of his skull. Diagnosis reported that there was no disturbance in the cranium only bleeding in the skull. After x-ray and tests of the skull and brain with treatment with of the bleeding, he was released back to his post.

After several weeks, Ensign 1966060412 had his first seizure. He encountered his first Grand Mal seizure that resulted in violent convulsion. The bridge went into disturbance. He was sitting near his console. His head struck the console so he bled due to the injury. He was brought to the infirmary for evaluation. Doctor Carl reported that any injury toward the cranium and its neural control was un-noticeable several weeks ago. He was given a treatment plan with medication and instructions. He was instructed to avoid strenuous physical work. Sitting at a console and monitoring it to give instructions to the crew will not be difficult. The bridge was given advice on how to deal with him should seizure occur; seizure may occur un-expectedly.

Ensign 1966060412 returned to his post and continued to do what he was trained to do. Ensign 1966060412 continued having Grand Mal seizures while we were in Quadrants A and B. He had several seizures on the bridge. He had seizures several times while traveling on the ship. The medications were not helping much. As a communications and network technician, he began to understand and simulate the nervous network with the communications network; he was also able to simulate the power network with the blood vessels. Understanding the seizures, he began to be able to lighten the types of seizures and lower the amounts by bringing confidence to himself and his body. He knew he cannot stop the seizures, but he can lighten the effects of the seizures on his regular routines.

Ensign 1966060412 continued to have Grand Mal seizures while in Quadrant B, but the amount of seizures had lessened. While in Quadrants C & D, his seizures had dropped from Grand Mal to Complex Partial. Complex Partial is mainly loss of consciousness. He would be noticed walking around and working consciously; but when people came up to him, he was found unconscious and sleep walking. A person just has to do what he plans to with self-awareness and conscious intelligence. The person will train his intelligence to instruct the un-conscious body and mind what the conscious person would do.

The ship-computer of the Jonathan is the entire vessel with its stations as a circuit points in the computer network. The crew is the self-aware consciousness of Jonathan and its advance computerized intelligence. The station consoles and the CNC processor will operate by the general plans and immediate plans the crew has worked with the ship to construct. The consoles and the CNC will do everything automatically by memorized plans making the ship computer a dead body. The crew is the life of the ship.

Direct instruction will be given to specific points in the infrastructure. Immediate plan of action of the station will trigger reflexive response triggering other station(s) to react predictably. Through experience the primary plan of operation of the structure, and the primary plan of action of the local station will be remembered. The immediate plan of action will be formulated from these factors along with other incoming variables and data.

Central control (officers and the captain at the bridge, the mind, brain and Central Nervous System at the cranium, and the CEO and executives at the head quarters office) will direct how the vessel will operate in the field and how the infrastructure of the vessel will operate internally to support the operation of the vessel. Central control will give directions to the stations all over the infrastructure how to operate. There is intension on how the stations in the infrastructure will influence the distribution of the power and supplies throughout the network of the vessel's autonomy. The operation and experience of the total vessel in field will manipulate how the points (stations) in the infrastructure of the vessel will operate, by response. The areas in the infrastructure of the structure will respond automatically and coherently. The momentum of the power distributions and the automatic responses will manipulate how the central control will respond with a direct message to the infrastructure.

As the Jonathan travels through Quadrant A and Quadrant B, the areas in the hull of this travelling vessel will operate and evolve. There is experience with the new environment in deep space. As the stations in the hull of the Jonathan receive direct message(s) on how to make changes and operate accordingly to adapt, the cellular points and motor areas all over the human body to move the whole body along with the construction and operation of the stations. After given the instruction on what is expected of the whole body to do in the environment of the hull, the cellular points in the body will be manipulated to operate and evolve coherently together. As the hull body of the vessel, and the anatomy of the human physiology changes, the infrastructure of the crew operation changes along.

Each station, each person, and unit will not be directly involved with each other's task. No party will be in involved in more than one task and be distracted. A party must be at its location and be experienced with its task as long as possible. This person will be able to formulate an understanding on how what to expect and how to do it. Whatever data this local station receives, he will know how to remember it by using the data and information consistently.

All areas and stations that are responsible in a specific field of operation will be connected with each other in a cloud to share their particular information. They will know how to use their specific data for specific field of purpose. An area may have more than one purpose. Data for the purpose will be shared with other stations and areas. All data and information from different locations, and different fields, will be organized and refined to the specific task of the station at the location. The clouds of different departments and fields of operation will formulate into one mass cloud of the vessel body or body or the organizational body.

The Jonathan evolves; the human body evolves; and the social organization and operation evolves. All points will work coherently with each other, directly and indirectly, to manipulate changes in the body and how the central will operate in the future. All this is by power momentum, and by message exchanges of the station-points and cellar points in the infrastructure of the body.

The CNC at the bridge, and CNS at the brain, does much work to monitor the control of the vessel body by the communicative neural network. Processing of the messages through the neural network will require power to do the work. The CNC on the bridge and the CNS in the brain will have to do much work in processing the entire neural network and stations of the vessel body will require much power. Should something is affecting the processing of the messages at the locations or delivery of the messages through the communicative neural network, much power will will be required; station(s) and power supplies will become exhausted.

The primary processor in the vessel body is the CNC or the CNS. It manages each station's processor through the communicative neural network. Should the primary processor and/or the neural network to the local processor are not operating effectively; the local station's processor will have to work coherently with the other stations' processors without central guidance. The stations will have to work harder and require more power than usual to work coherently with the other stations in their vessel body.

Operational Order

The UFS Jonathan is on a diplomatic mission. It is not to make contaminate to culture or the environment. Before entering atmosphere of the planet, we are to gather data to determine how we can enter the environment without contaminating it. We will also learn how to protect ourselves from contamination from the environment, from the data gathered.

Before we began taking 'away' missions onto the planet, we had to go through drills to train ourselves on how to get involved with other cultures. We will learn to be diplomatic with ourselves; then will we learn how to be diplomatic with others. We have to overcome stress due to isolation and time. We will be away from civilization for a long time. We have to create a culture environment on the Jonathan. The Jonathan must have pleasurable resting quarters (not fancy quarters). There must also be pleasurable lounges for the crew to associate with each other off duty. Jonathan must become a large housing facility or a city in space.

It has been a month since we entered into Quadrant B. The crew has learned to adapt and accept each others' personal differences. We approached Planet Quadrant B 123. Data has revealed that it is not habitable. There are no sentient life, no animal life and no plant life. The atmosphere is very dense and protective suits are suggested. The gravity of the planet is very heavy so protective suit is definite. The materials on the planet are rich in resources for power and supplies.

The 'away' team consisted of the Exec Officer, the Science Officer, the Engineering Officer, Engineering Technician Lt. 6606362082, and crewmember 7183888003 (the Traveler). The shuttle bay was a quarantined area. Their bodies and their suits had to be decontaminated before the 'away' team entered into their suits and then enter onto the shuttle bay. The shuttle had to be decontaminated also before they boarded. The shuttle, the suits, and the bodies must be adaptable to the planet and its environment so there will be no contamination (contamination to themselves or contamination to the environment).

Landing onto Quadrant B 123 was no different than any landing we experienced in training in Earth's star system. Walking onto the planet ground was a sensational feeling; walking onto a planet ground far from Earth's Quadrant. The Cmd. Johns directed the Lt. Cmd. Kevin to walk with crewmember 7183888003 to gather materials from the ground for tests to be made on the planet; and make scientific observations (reports of the planet). Lt. Cmd. Mat was instructed to walk with crewmember 6606362082 to start testing on the materials for the type of power source present. An immediate field lab was constructed before the field teams went out for their data.

The 'away' mission was brief, several days. We made detailed reports of the planets conditions, and its resources. There was no dangerous risk on the planet. Cmd. Johns remarked that Planet Quadrant B 123 was so rich in resources that it would be a dream of a mining company; but Planet Earth is no longer a commercializing civilization but a searcher of knowledge and friends.

We left Planet Quadrant B 123 peacefully. We entered into a quarantined shuttle bay. We left the shuttle and stepped onto the bay with our suits on. The bay was undergoing decontamination so the bay was in a vacuum. We entered into a quarantine area for personnel to stay without their clothes on. We stayed in the quarantine area for several days undergoing decontamination. We were isolated from the crew but did not feel isolated. We kept in communication with the crew through the communication console. The Exec prepared his mission report while the Science Officer prepared hers and the Engineering Officer prepared hers.

After entering into Quadrant C, the first planet we encountered and chose to study was Quadrant C 345. Data obtained from orbital probes showed that the planet was habitable with a very comfortable environment; it would make a lovely vacation area for leave. The planet was rich with usable resources. This planet was also occupied with a civilization so we have to be careful. Avoiding contamination of the environment is no hard work; but avoiding contamination of a culture will be.

The 'away' team was lead by Cmd. Johns. He chose the Science Officer, the Counselor, the Doctor, the Engineering Officer, and crewmember 7183888003 for his team. Before we land, the Captain chose to make a longer observation of the planet and its culture before we do anything.

The orbiting probes showed that the civilization was advance with advance technology. The people were very friendly; they were friendly toward each other and toward the animal life and plant life surrounding them. The strange thing was how were they operating the technology and how was the technology being powered.

We decided to land and make contact. We decided to enter the atmosphere and land distant from the community inconspicuously. We will enter into the community inconspicuously and become part of the community. We entered into the community and were divided into our separate teams. Cmd. Johns joined Lt. Cmd. Simmons to find their library and their leadership facility. Lt. Cmd. Carl went to the local medical facility to find information on their physiology. Crewmember 7183888003 joined Lt. Cmd. Mat and Lt. Cmd. Kevin to locate the power facility to learn about their power source and means of power distribution. We chose the gateway to the city as our meeting place in 3 days.

The Exec and the Counselor looked around and could not find any library, any books, any computer console or even a community hall. The Exec and the Counselor were confused. What confused them more were how the people were walking slowly and calm, as if nothing was happening? When they made facial contact, it was not Johns and Simmons who were studying them but it was they who were studying the officers with confusion and curiosity. They walked but they did not talk.

The Doctor searched for a medical facility but could not find one. He decided to make a medical evaluation of one of the residents. He used his hand held medical detector to review the residents passing by. He pointed at each individual he encountered and found that their physical bodies were operating autonomously and calmly. It appeared as if there were no defects in their body. Each person may have different physical appearances, but their physiology performed the same way. The Doctor then pointed the medical detector into the air and found that there were no indifferences in the air. He eventually made the diagnosis that everybody on the planet were perfectly healthy and that the environment was perfectly pure and healthy. The Doctor thought to himself, "They do not talk but how do they communicate."

Lt. Cmd. Mat, Lt. Cmd. Kevin and crewmember 7183888003 tried to locate a central power station but couldn't find one. They then approached a home and found that it had a power generating box of its own. The generator box was constructed and operated like a mass power station that produced quantum power. Their engine was no different than ours except that it was small and could be held at the palm of the hand. They went to several homes and other facilities and found that each place had a similar power source.

After several days and many facial contacts, the separate teams joined at the gateway of the city. We shared notes about what we had found. Our different hypothesis shared the same variable; the people were slow, calm, and curious but are not talking. We tried to come to the speculation that they were impaired. A question came up; how could impaired individuals create and operate a community of such advance technology (technology more advance than ours)?

Suddenly, one of the people came to us. He greeted us with how we find their city and civilization. They then began talking to each other. This person who greeted us told us that they were confused of our presence. He said we were different from them and did not perform as they did so they had to stay calm study our behaviors to know how to relate with us.

The Counselor and the Doctor concluded that the people were very advance and could communicate telepathically. Our first encounter with them only showed that they were impaired in response, not impaired in thought or reasoning. They wish to know and understand what they are about to encounter before they make any responses. Each individual was studying us through their physical senses. Then they shared their gathered information and studied us together with the non tangible 6th sense.

The occupants of Planet Quadrant C 345 use all 6 of their senses to their full capacity. Their technology is very advance, more advance than ours. They were once able to travel deep space with quantum power. Their quantum engines were once large. They have advanced beyond that. They no long travel into deep space to study the other worlds. They study the visitors and their planets through the visitors' minds, thoughts and behaviors. Their archive memory and the surface memory are one allowing them to reason and remember past and present deeply. They will not make direct contact until they have studied their visitor(s).

Their value for trade is the quantum power they use physically in their advance community; and the knowledge they will gather and share together. Like the Jonathan, each station learns individually and shares their data with each other through the CNC. The stations and the CNC become one computer and respond toward the speculation made. The occupants of Planet Quadrant C 345 form the infrastructure of the civilization. They receive their allowance of knowledge and resources through the infrastructure. From their allowances, they give back some to the infrastructure to maintain the infrastructure. Jonathan's daily performance simulates this quality.

At Quadrant D, we came to Planet Quadrant D 456. Orbital probes found that the planet atmosphere was fairly habitable; the atmosphere was a bit light and hot. The planet was molten; volcanic. It appeared that the planet is young. To avoid contamination to the planet and to ourselves, data had to be gathered so we can find means to adapt.

We landed near the mountains. The Science Officer, the Doctor and crewmember 7183888003 were the 'away' team. We did not wear any protective suiting so we felt the heat and the humidity. We walked around to gather data together. We came to a pool of molten gel. The detector detected hydrocarbon and methane in this carbon based gel; it is similar to petroleum. This pool was mass, as large as the planet. Cmd. Carl and Lt. Cmd. Kevin concluded that the carbon base gel is the founding factor for carbon based organic life. Evolutionary life is about to begin. We must not interfere with evolution. We have found the perfect facility to study our past ancestry by studying this planet; but we must study this planet from a distance away and never disturb it.

If the civilization present is distant from us in culture and technology, don't get involved or make contact. This 'organ' is not fully prepared for the infrastructure of the body. If the organ wishes to evolve and get involved in the infrastructure, let it find its own way to. Let the resources come to the organ and let the organ capture and use the resources on its own. If the organ cannot evolve on its own, it cannot join the infrastructure and contribute to it.

Make contact with the organ or culture, this organ becomes a station-point in the infrastructure. Fellow station-points in the infrastructure will assist each other to maintain the autonomy of the infrastructure, but they will not interfere with each other's responsibilities and performances.

After studying several planets in Quadrant D, we returned to our home star system, to the Alpha Station. We have much to report. Each crewmember will provide a duty report. Crewmember 7183888003 will provide a summary journal along with his duty report.

The UFS Jonathan produces much power to use. Power will come fast. The stations and areas all around the vessel must be ready to use the mass amount of power being provided. The neural network must be prepared to guide the stations to cooperate with each other in using the power. If the stations or the network are not prepared for the power provided, the local stations and the whole vessel will begin to operate chaotically and erratically. The power packets must be prepared to deliver the mass amount of power or they will not be able to carry and deliver the sufficient amount of power the stations are prepared and are ready to use.

Like the newly born Siberian Lynx running around in the field playing and learning, the newly commissioned UFS Jonathan is experiencing Quadrant A to learn about its potentials and limits. The crew of the Jonathan is learning about its vessel's potentials and limits; and learns about their own potentials and limits.

Venture begins with a general plan of operation. Each station, each area, and each individual, will construct its own immediate plan of action which may eventually become its own general plan of action. It will be used with the incoming information to construct a new plan of action. Use a plan with the information to construct a plan and the information will not be forgotten.

A republic is a dominion consisting of an autonomous infrastructure of sovereignties. A station-point, organ or individual is sovereignty. The central basis that holds this dominion and infrastructure together is a system of operation. This system is kept together by communication and distribution of resources. Distribution is by free trade. The federation or federal is the central system, not an individual sovereignty.

Free trade is the life and strength of the infrastructure, the infrastructural system. The infrastructural system consists of the central order of the trade flow by a federal trade (central maintenance) and direct trade amongst the points in the infrastructure. The federal center of the infrastructure is the system and directive that the organization exists and operates by. The Federal Republic is not a dictatorship controlled by one. It is a system in the infrastructure where all station-points are part of; all station-points will operate coherently together in accordance to a doctrine. There will be no difference in equality and respect. The only difference is in levels of responsibilities and tasks; the greater the responsibility and task, the higher the allowance to provide for what is needed and what is rewarded.

Provisions will be provided through a system of free trade and cooperative responsibility in the infrastructure. Provisions will be distributed through the allowances given to each party. Allowances will be in trade credits. Free trade must be kept to keep the resources flowing. Free trade will be by direct bartering, and by federal trade. Direct bartering will be by direct contact with trading parties. Points that cannot participate with free trade route will be assisted by the federal trade to keep them up to date to participate with the free trade.

From the allowance, each party (each station-point) will get what it needs, what it wants, and give back, invest back, to the federal trade to assist fellow members of the infrastructure. The strength of the infrastructure is coherency and cooperation through free trade and communication. To ensure coherency, all sovereignties are equal. Their only differences are their different levels of responsibilities and performances. The hierarchy is in the responsibilities, task and performance; not by position and privileges. Allowances will be given for what is needed in the responsibilities and rewarded for the efforts given.

> *"Money is like manure. It's not worth a thing unless it's spread about, encouraging young things to grow."*[22]

The federal trade system is the central maintenance of the infrastructure. If nothing is given back to the system, eventually there will be nothing left to maintain the system, the infrastructure, or the autonomy of the structure. Disrupt the traffic of the provisions, and disrupt the communication of the parties in the infrastructure, there will be no more coherency or cooperation in the infrastructure. If there is no infrastructure, there is no longer an autonomous structure. If this happens, then 'Firehall' has just happened. It will take much to rebuild this autonomous structure.

> *Resources (power source, materials, support) will be gathered to be refined and used by the body.*
> *Resources are refined into fuel and power (power, supplies, social support, fiscal support and personnel support) to be shared and used amongst the residents (work stations, motor areas, departments and indigenous parts) of the body.*
> *All residents of the body will maintain communication with each other to work coherently and cooperatively together.*

---

[22] Quote from the play *"Hello Dolly"*.

Eco-Balance (Ecological Balance; Economical Balance) is the system that maintains the infrastructure of the autonomous body. Each organ/station/ individual is a consumer, a producer, and a distributor. Each will take, give back, and provide directly and indirectly to fellow participants in the infrastructure. The system must be kept in circulation and in operation at all times. Suspension of the system will lead to the suspension of the infrastructure. Suspension of the autonomous body's infrastructure will cause severe damage to the body and probably terminating it.

A general plan on what the organization is for and how it shall operate will be specified and understood. From the general plan of operation, immediate plans of operation will be constructed to the template of the general plan and the variables present affecting the operation. From the immediate plans of operation will construct the general plan of action for each area, each organ of the organization.

The DNA is the general map of the physical living body; the primary directive that the civilization (the organization) exists and functions by is the general map of the organization. The infrastructure is the structural design of the organization's body. The directive determines how each point in the infrastructure will develop and operate. The primary directive is the center of the federal order of the infrastructure that the organization exists and operates by. General plans of operation, and general plans of action, will be constructed in accordance to the primary directive of the organization.

> An immediate plan of action will be constructed in accordance to the general plan of action template and the variable(s) that the organ is encountering. The immediate plan of action from each area/organ will become the variable(s) that will affect the construction of the immediate plan of operation. The immediate plan of operation may become a general plan of operation in accordance to the ultimate plan of what the organization is and how the organization will deal with what is, maybe, expected.

Firehall:

> ➤ *Stage 1*   ***Disruption of the structure's routines causing suspension in the gathering of resources.***
> ➤ *Stage 2*   ***Suspension of the trade and distribution of fuel and power amongst the residents of the body.***
> ➤ *Stage 3*   ***Suspension of the communication network amongst the residents will damage coherency and cooperation to enable restoration of the damaged body.***

Devastation, manmade or natural, brings malnutrition and great loss. Distribution of food, housing, power, and allowances will be disrupted. The infrastructure is crippled but not destroyed yet. Once communication and coherency is gone, the infrastructure is gone. Should any area in the infrastructure is damaged by devastation the other areas of the infrastructure must make sacrifices in their allowances to help the crippled area recover.

The response is only as good as the reception. Disruption in the traffic and communication will impair the response and coherency, within the infrastructure, and the structure. The autonomous structure may have to slow down and improvise to enable the damaged area to recover and strengthen the infrastructure. Recovery is better than replacement. It will take much more time for replacement to adapt then the repaired to.

The human civilization on planet Earth is a vessel and crew traveling in deep space. The communities and societies in Earth form the infrastructure of the human civilization on Earth. If any part of the infrastructure experiences devastation, the other parts of the infrastructure (the communities and societies) will have to provide allowances to the area in need. If the structure of the civilization is to continue to exist, the infrastructure of the civilization must regain strength; the damaged area must recover and give to the infrastructure again.

If situation has occurred causing effect on the transportation and trading of resources, and the communication network to maintain the trafficking, trading and the usage of the resources productively, immediate means to restore the infrastructure must be made before the infrastructure is totally damaged beyond repair.

> ➤ *Communication must be restored to the fullest to enable cooperation.*
> ➤ *From the communication amongst all involved, there must come to an agreement on what is needed and how they will be used for the survival of the autonomous body.*
> ➤ *Once agreeing to what is needed internally, there must be an agreement to where the resources for what is needed will come from and how they will arrive.*

All in an alliance will work coherently together forming a strong infrastructure. There will be competition with fellow allies to determine who can perform better for the infrastructure. The competition(s) bring attention to the need(s) for better results. Reward that brings attention to improvements is an accelerating reward and is truly the victory sought after. If there is no accelerating reward, there is no victory.

Avoid all confrontations until all is known. Confront the problem but don't get involved in aggression/conflict. Aggression brings no accelerating reward so there is no victory in aggression; there is no victory in war. The members of the infrastructure of the human civilization must overcome their aggression toward each other. There will always be competitive reverie amongst friends and allies to show achievement(s), but they needn't be aggressive.

The competition will be the attempt to show better in strength, courage, wisdom, intelligence, and wealth. The best way to show strength, wisdom, and courage is not by how well one can fight; but putting aside his pride and emotions knowing when to act and how to act. The best way to show wisdom, knowledge and wealth is not how much one has; but how well one can use what he has. Many things can be used in many ways besides aggression. Defense can be by reconstruction and development of the impaired instead of aggressing and combating with each other.

An efficiently managed ship and organization will not have the organization exist as a dictatorship. It may be run as a dominion with each station (sovereignty) treating each other with equal respect and privileges. It will not be a dictatorship dominated by only a few or the one to the prominent respect and privileges.

The superior (greater in responsibilities) respects the junior (lesser in responsibilities) as the junior respects the superiors. All individuals and all stations require each other for the efficient operation of the ship. All will provide assistance to each other in the ship. One of the most needed assistance and activity is circulation of the resources. Even the rural stations will come out to full activity and provide assistance where needed in restoration and regeneration of the vessel body.

There is to be no bias. Individuals will not be designated by race, color, gender, age, class or ethnicity. Individuals will only be designated their qualification, performance and assignment. Individuals will be rotated in accordance where needed. Individuals do not need to like each other to work with each other. The goal to maintain the infrastructure and the autonomy of the civilization/organization is all that is needed to work with enthusiasm.

The world has evolved through the centuries. The field has changed many times so the human body changes with it. One only reaps what the field has allowed sown.

The human body consists of many organs and many cells. Should anything happen to his body all organs and all cells will work together to repair the damage and recover.

What is the purpose for the internal conflict in the body of mankind? We must work together to restore from the damage done.

Restore by moving on and build from what was lost. Learn from what had happened and work together to build on from there.

We must work together as one collective mind and body or we haven't learned a thing.

The greatest wonder is brotherly love shown through combined-joint effort.

FDA'S APPROVAL OF SPIRULINA

A I B M R
Life Sciences, Inc.

Division of Biotechnology and GRAS Notice Review
Office of Food Additive Safety-CFSAN
U.S. Food and Drug Administration
5100 Paint Branch Parkway (HFS-255)
College Park, MD 20740-3835

July 12, 2011

ATTN: Dr. Antonia Mattia, PhD

Our Reference: GRAS Notification and Exemption Claim for Certified Organic Spirulina

Dear Dr. Mattia,

AIBMR Life Sciences, Inc. has been retained as an agent by E.I.D. Parry (India) Limited, Parry Nutraceuticals Division ('the Notifier') to submit a GRAS notification to the FDA for Certified Organic Spirulina, a powdered preparation of organically grown *Arthrospira platensis* to be used as an ingredient in the enclosed specified categories of food.

Please find enclosed three copies of the notification *Notice to US Food and Drug Administration that the use of Certified Organic Spirulina (Arthrospira platensis) is Generally Recognized as Safe*. As stated in the exemption claim, the data and the information that serve as the basis for this GRAS determination will be available for review and copying at reasonable times at the office of Parry Nutraceuticals Division, E.I.D Parry (India) Ltd., "Dare House" No.234, N.S.C Bose Road, Chennai – 600 001, India; or will be sent to FDA upon request.

Parry Nutraceuticals (the notifier), has determined that Certified Organic Spirulina is Generally Regarded as Safe (GRAS), consistent with section 201 (s) of the Federal Food, Drug and Cosmetic Act. This determination has been made based on scientific procedures, and includes reference to FDA GRAS notification No. 127, which was filed for Spirulina in 2003. Spirulina has a long history of human consumption and has been thoroughly researched in toxicological models, with no results prompting concern for safety. It has been recommended as a food for human consumption by governmental agencies. In summary, the use of Certified Organic Spirulina in the enclosed specified categories of food is exempt from the requirement of pre-market approval.

Yours sincerely,

John R. Endres
Chief Scientific Officer
AIBMR Life Sciences, Inc.
john@aibmr.com

4117 SOUTH MERIDIAN
PUYALLUP, WA 98373

(253) 286-2888 PH
(253) 286-2451

WWW.AIBMR.COM

Notice to US Food and Drug Administration that the use of Certified Organic Spirulina (*Arthrospira platensis*) is Generally Recognized as Safe

Submitted by the Notifier:

E.I.D. Parry (India) Limited,
Parry Nutraceuticals Division,
"Dare House"
No.234, N.S.C Bose Road,
Chennai – 600 001, India

Prepared by the Agent of the Notifier:

AIBMR Life Sciences, Inc
4117 S Meridian
Puyallup WA 98373

July 12th, 2011

Table of Contents

1. GRAS Exemption Claim

E.I.D. Parry (India) Limited, Parry Nutraceuticals Division (the notifier), in consultation with an independent panel of experts qualified by scientific training and experience to evaluate the safety of ingredients intended for use in food, has determined that Certified Organic Spirulina is Generally Recognized as Safe (GRAS) for its intended use, consistent with section 201 (s) of the Federal Food, Drug and Cosmetic Act. The determination has been made based on scientific procedures, and therefore the use of Organic Spirulina for its intended use is exempt from the requirement of pre-market approval.

(b) (6)

29th Jun 2011

Dr. L. Rajendran
Head, Quality Assurance
E.I.D. Parry (India) Limited
Parry Nutraceuticals Division

Date

(i) Name and Address of the Notifier

a. Notifier

E.I.D. Parry (India) Limited,
Parry Nutraceuticals Division,
"Dare House"
No.234, N.S.C Bose Road,
Chennai – 600 001, India

b. Agent of the Notifier

John R. Endres, ND
Chief Scientific Officer
AIBMR Life Sciences, Inc.
4117 S. Meridian
Puyallup, WA 98373
Tel: (253) 286-2888 x101; Fax: (253) 286-2451
john@aibmr.com

(ii) Common or Usual Name

Certified Organic Spirulina (a powdered preparation of organically grown *Arthrospira platensis*)

(iii) Conditions of Use

Certified Organic Spirulina is intended for use at levels of 0.5–3 grams per serving, as an ingredient in the following food categories; *beverages and beverage bases* (nonalcoholic, including only special or spiced teas, soft drinks, coffee substitutes, and fruit and vegetable flavored gelatin drinks); *breakfast cereals* (including ready-to-eat and instant and regular hot cereals); *fresh fruits and fruit juices* (including only raw fruits, citrus, melons, and berries, and home-prepared "ades" and punches made therefrom); *frozen dairy desserts and mixes* (including ice cream, ice milks, sherbets, and other frozen dairy desserts and specialties); *grain products and pastas* (including macaroni and noodle products, rice dishes, and frozen multicourse meals, without meat or vegetables); *milk products* (including flavored milks and milk drinks, dry milks, toppings, snack dips, spreads, weight control milk beverages, and other milk origin products); *plant protein products* (including the National Academy of Sciences/National Research Council "reconstituted vegetable protein" category, and meat, poultry, and fish substitutes, analogs, and extender products made from plant proteins); *processed fruits and fruit juices* (including all commercially processed fruits, citrus, berries, and mixtures; salads, juices and juice punches, concentrates, dilutions, "ades", and drink substitutes made therefrom); *processed vegetables and vegetable juices* (including all commercially processed vegetables, vegetable dishes, frozen multicourse vegetable meals, and vegetable juices and blends) *snack foods* (including chips, pretzels, and other novelty snacks); *soft candy* (including candy bars, chocolates, fudge, mints, and other chewy or nougat candies); and *soups and soup mixes* (including commercially prepared meat, fish, poultry (at levels that fall within FDA jurisdiction), vegetable, and combination soups and soup mixes).

(iv) Basis for GRAS determination

Scientific procedures are the basis for this GRAS determination.

(v) Data/Information Availability Statement

The data and the information that serve as the basis for this GRAS determination will be available for review and copying at reasonable times at the office of Parry Nutraceuticals Division, E.I.D Parry (India) Ltd., "Dare House" No.234, N.S.C Bose Road, Chennai – 600 001, India; or will be sent to FDA upon request.

2. Characterization

Certified Organic Spirulina is Parry Nutraceuticals' spray dried powder consisting of whole, dry cells of *Arthrospira platensis*; a cyanobacterium commonly known as "Spirulina". True Spirulina is in fact a different genus; however all the edible forms that are under commercial cultivation and sold as Spirulina actually belong to the Genus *Arthrospira* (Tomaselli *et al.*). Since *Arthrospira* is commonly marketed with the trade name Spirulina, and since Spirulina is the name used commercially, this report uses the two interchangeably with the understanding that Certified Organic Spirulina and other commercially produced Spirulina are strains of *Arthrospira*. Parry's source strain for Spirulina culture was obtained from the Indian Agricultural Research Institute (IARI), New Delhi culture collection. The IARI strain has been taxonomically identified and verified as non-GMO *A. platensis* (Desikachary *et al.* 1996). This species and strain of filamentous cyanobacteria is presumably from Chad. Other *Arthrospira* species and strains are found in other tropical and sub-tropical water bodies in Africa, Asia, and South America.

A. platensis is one of three commonly cultivated and investigated *Arthrospira* cyanobacterium species. The other two are *A. maxima* and *A. fusiformis*. All three are frequently referred to by the traditional names of *Spirulina platensis, Spirulina maxima,* and *Spirulina fusiformis*. Microscopically, they appear as blue-green filaments composed of cylindrical cells arranged in unbranched, helicoidal trichomes. The main morphological feature of the genus is the open left hand helix arrangement along the entire length of the multicellular trichomes. The slight differences between the species are mainly related to the architecture of the trichomes. For instance, *A. maxima's* trichomes, as compared to the trichomes of *A. platensis*, are often wider in diameter, attenuated at the ends, and less constricted at the crosswalls (Vonshak 1997).

However, different growth and stress conditions cause morphological elasticity variations among these species, causing confusion among the scientific community concerning species nomenclature. According to Tomaselli, in *Spirulina platensis (Arthrospira): Physiology, Cell-biology, and Biotechnology*, it remains uncertain whether *A. maxima* and *A. fusiformis* can be considered separate species from *A. platensis* (Vonshak 1997; Scheldeman *et al.* 1999). For this reason, toxicological studies using various strains and even species, such as *A. maxima*, are considered when determining safety profiles.

Arthrospira species have recently undergone reclassification. The most current and authoritative work in bacterial taxonomy uses a new classification system based on phylogenetic lines instead of morphology (Garrity 2005).

Chemical Composition

Certified Organic Spirulina is a fine, uniform powder, blue-green to green in color, with a mild odor and taste. It is unique in its chemical composition because of its high nutritional density; it contains a wide range and abundance of macro- and micronutrients, as well as phytochemicals. In terms of macronutrients, Certified Organic Spirulina contains high levels of protein (56–69%) with a balanced amino acid profile, 15–25% carbohydrates (mainly glucose), and 5–6% lipids, mainly as polyunsaturated fatty acids with a high ratio of gamma-linolenic acid (GLA). The micronutrient composition features relatively high concentrations of B-vitamins, especially cyanocobalamin (0.05–0.20 mg/100g). Spirulina's phytonutrient composition includes phycocyanins (phycobiliproteins involved in light harvesting reactions), carotenes (including beta-carotene), chlorophyll, and xanthophylls. Batches of Certified Organic Spirulina are routinely assayed in Parry Nutraceuticals' Quality Assurance Lab for protein, moisture, total ash (minerals), bulk density, light filth, algal (microcystin) toxins and microbes in addition to the phytopigments listed above (see Table 3 in section 3 (iv) a., entitled specifications and batch analyses).

Organic Certification

In addition to USDA National Organic Program (NOP) organic standards, Parry Nutraceuticals cultivates Certified Organic Spirulina under a number of other major international organic standards: Naturland (Germany), ECOCERT certification (France), and OCIA -USA (Organic Crop Improvement Association). The product is also certified Kosher (Star K) and Halal.

Parry Nutraceuticals' Spirulina is certified by USP under the USP Ingredient Verification Program—meeting USP specifications for GMP, manufacturing, quality control documentation, and label claims. These accredited organizations are world leaders in the certification of organic products, and their certifications guarantee conformity and traceability to American, European, or other standards.

3.   Manufacturing and Production

(i)   Company Overview

Parry Nutraceuticals, has a twenty-year history of research and development in micro-algal biotechnology. The company manufactures and produces USDA National Organic Program Certified Organic Spirulina at their production facility located in Oonaiyur, in South India. The 120-acre facility is located in a remote area where temperatures and climate are conducive to Spirulina production (21–39° Celsius, intense sunlight, minimal precipitation), where there is no ground water contamination, and where there is no other agricultural activity—eliminating the possibility of artificial fertilizer or pesticide contamination. The mass production of Certified Organic Spirulina utilizes the open-pond, or raceway pond system which was developed in the 1950's and is widely used for outdoor mass cultivation of photosynthetic microorganisms. The production facility at Oonaiyur has twenty-nine acres of raceway ponds, including production ponds and two evaporation ponds with a capacity of 19,000 cubic meters. The facility also houses two pump/processing houses, an effluent treatment plant to meet the Pollution Control Board's requirements, a granulation and packing facility, a finished product warehouse, a raw materials storehouse, and a laboratory. The facility meets FDA GMP standards as demonstrated by Parry Nutraceuticals' United States Pharmacopeia (USP) certification for dietary supplements.

All of Parry Nutraceuticals' products comply with all applicable regulations and directives of the USA, EU and other nations on non-genetically modified, non-allergen, non-irradiation, transmissible and bovine spongiform encephalopathy (TSE/BSE), dioxins, polychlorinated biphenyl (PCB), and traceability. Parry Nutraceuticals' products are currently exported to over thirty-five countries in North America, South East Asia and Western Europe, including the USA.

(ii) Raw Materials

Along with the Spirulina inoculum, the raw materials used in the manufacturing of Certified Organic Spirulina include water, inoculation nutrients, and pond cultivation nutrients. The inoculation and pond cultivation nutrients, discussed below, consist of sea salt and organic nutrients of plant origin. The materials are purchased from approved vendors. All materials must arrive with supporting documents. Incoming raw materials are inspected, sampled, and stored in designated raw material storage houses. Random samples of 2% of the number of containers received are sent to Parry Nutraceuticals' in-house laboratory or approved outside laboratories where they are tested and verified by designated authorities.

Water

The water used at Parry Nutraceuticals for the cultivation and processing of Spirulina is drawn from a series of bore wells within the 120-acre facility. The bore well water is softened to less than 100 ppm hardness for use in the production process and run through PVC piping. After the algal biomass has been pumped from the ponds and pre-filtered, water (with no additives or processing aids) is also used for washing the harvested algal biomass in the concentrator.

Water samples are tested daily for physical appearance and hardness and monthly for microbiological contamination. Water is also tested once every six months for heavy metals. A 100–250 mL random sample is sent to an accredited laboratory identified by Parry Nutraceuticals and analyzed for arsenic, cadmium, lead and mercury per AOAC 2000 protocols. Acceptable limits are per the specification sheets provided by Parry Nutraceuticals.

Inoculation Nutrients

Raw materials are added at two stages of production: the initial (indoor) inoculation stage and the outdoor raceway pond cultivation stage (see "Production" section below).

The raw materials used for the initial inoculation stage are added to distilled water and the Spirulina inoculum. These materials constitute the inoculation medium, known as the Modified Zarrouk Medium. The nutrients for preparing the Modified Zarrouk Medium are listed in Table 1. The concentrations are per 1 liter distilled water.

Table 1. Modified Zarrouk Medium

Organic nitrogen source	5.0 g
Sea salt	1.0 g

Pond Cultivation Nutrients

The raw materials used for the outdoor cultivation of Certified Organic Spirulina consist of organic vegetable-origin fertilizers (normally code named as "PN" for Plant Nutrients) water, and sea salt. The PN utilized are certified organic as per USDA and Ecocert organic standards and are certified for use in organic agriculture. They are obtained from a non-genetically modified legume seeds oil seed extraction process, and are added to the production ponds on a need basis (see Production section below). Varying amounts are added to the ponds when required, in order to optimize the biomass density and health and to prevent the growth of contaminants.

Sea salt is also added to the production ponds on a need basis. The sea salt is purchased from an approved vendor and must demonstrate purity. An approved laboratory is used to analyze the moisture content, sodium chloride content, other soluble and insoluble matter, and aluminum silicate content. The sea salt is also analyzed for heavy metals, as described above for all raw materials.

(iii) Manufacturing Overview

Parry Nutraceuticals cultivation and production process is certified under ISO 9001 (quality management systems), ISO 14001 (environmental management systems), and ISO 22000 (food safety management systems). Quality systems have been established to ensure that all of the algal products produced meet the requirements established in food GMP (CFR part 110).

Parry Nutraceuticals' production process follows the open raceway pond design developed in the 1950's and widely used for the outdoor mass cultivation of photosynthetic microorganisms. This process involves indoor and then semi-outdoor cultivation of the Spirulina culture, followed by outdoor pond cultivation, harvesting, washing, drying, packing, warehousing and shipping. The entire production process is designed and carefully monitored to encourage *A. platensis* growth and prevent contamination.

Cultivation

The initial indoor cultivation involves growing Spirulina culture in sterile flasks under artificial lights in the prescribed organic medium, which consists of distilled water and the raw materials discussed previously. It is then progressively cultured and sub-cultured, first in flasks and then in larger plastic tubs. The outdoor cultivation involves the inoculation of tub cultures into a seed pond, followed by the progressive inoculation of other seed ponds until a certain level of biomass is met, at which time this culture is used to inoculate ½-acre production ponds. This organic production pond is then sub-cultured again into ponds earmarked for Spirulina production. The production ponds may contain varying volumes of culture depending on the pond depth. The ponds are agitated by paddle wheels in order to facilitate light distribution and nutrient distribution, minimize self-shading due to buoyancy, and maintain a uniform temperature. Nutrients (as listed under Raw Materials), and soft water are added to the ponds, which are agitated daily.

Pond Maintenance and Monitoring

The maintenance and monitoring of the ponds involves daily culture medium testing (sample collection, pond depth maintenance, optical density, and pH), microscopy, chemical analysis, and meteorological notation (temperature, sunshine duration, and rainfall). After agitating for two hours, a 50 mL culture sample is collected daily from a marked place in all ponds. From the sample, optical density is measured using a spectrophotometer in order to estimate biomass density. (The timing of the culturing and sub-culturing process, in which the Spirulina culture is inoculated in a series of progressively larger tubs and ponds, is based on the optical density.) The pH is measured using a pH meter. Microscopy is also performed daily. A drop of culture from each pond is examined microscopically for contamination by other algae, rotifers, zooplanktons, motile flagellates, and precipitates. In addition, the health and size of the trichomes, which are *Arthrospira's* distinguishing morphological feature (and described in more detail earlier in this document), are determined daily via microscopy. Chemical analysis of the culture medium is done on an as-needed basis and includes testing for nitrogen, phosphorous, sulfur, bicarbonate, and carbonate using standard methods. Spirulina is selected for harvest based on the pond's biomass levels, the culture medium testing, and the microscopy results.

Harvesting and Packaging

The harvesting, washing, and drying of the Spirulina begins with cleaning all process lines, sumps, tanks, machines, pipes, other equipment, and rooms. The culture is then pumped from the ponds to the process building where it is pre-filtered, and then sent through a concentrator for washing with water. The collected algal biomass is stored in tanks and cooled by a water-cooling system until ready for drying. It is then spray dried meeting all food quality standards. Finally, it is collected and packaged under nitrogen or vacuum packed in multi-layer food-grade poly bags. The bags are stored in carton boxes that have been tagged with a batch number. The cartons are stacked in a place designated for Organic Spirulina in a separate finished product warehouse kept free of moisture and contamination.

(iv) Specifications, Batch Analysis and Quality Management

a.   Specifications and Batch Analyses

Production consistency is tested in production lots. As shown in Table 3 below, four non-sequential batches were reasonably consistent and met the product specifications for physical/general composition, phytopigments, heavy metals, microbial analyses and absence of microcystin completely.

Table 3: Specifications and Batch Analysis of Organic Spirulina

Parameter	Specification	Method	Lot Numbers			
			PS-0424-VNK/10-11	PS-0425-VNK/10-11	PS-0531-VNK/10-11	PS-0532-VNK/10-11
Physical Properties/General Composition						
Protein (% dry wt)	56–69	AOAC 978.04 16th Edition	62.14	62.20	62.05	62.10
Moisture (% dry wt)	2.5–6.0	AOAC 934.01 16th Edition	4.20	4.15	4.2	4.15
Total Ash (Minerals) (% dry wt)	6.0–9.0	AOAC 930.05 16th Edition	6.99	7.02	6.90	7.10
Bulk Density (g/cc)	0.62–0.85	C.Vijayaraghavan (1995). A Practical handbook of physical pharmaceutics, 1995.	0.769	0.769	0.769	0.769
Phytopigments						
Total Carotenoids (mg/100 g dry wt)	400–650	Strickland and Parsons (1972). A practical Handbook of Seawater Analysis	425	434	426	420
Beta Carotene (mg/100 g dry wt)	150–250	Ranganna S. (1986). Handbook of analysis and QC for fruit & veg. Products.	162	165	164	162
Xanthophylls (mg/100 g dry wt)	250–470	In house method	263	269	262	258
Crude Phycocyanin (% dry wt)	15–19	Boussiba, S, Arch. Microbiol, 120:155 – 159, 1979	16.57	16.62	16.44	16.37
Chlorophyll-a (% dry wt)	1.23–1.67	Vonshak.A.1997. Spirulina platensis (Arthrospira) physiology, cell biology and biotechnology.	1.48	1.49	1.42	1.39
Total Pheophorbide (% dry wt)	≤ 0.12	A. Test method for Spirulina by JHFA, Environmental Food Number 99 (1981).	0.019	0.021	0.021	0.022
Existing Pheophorbide (% dry wt)	≤ 0.08	B. Seward R. Brown. Absorption Coefficients of Chlorophyll Derivatives. J.Fish. Res. BdCanada 25 (3) 523 – 540, 1968	0.017	0.019	0.020	0.020
Light Filth (pieces/50g)	≤ 50	Richard Gorham. J. (1977). Training manual for Analytical Entomology in the food industry. FDA Tech. Bulletin No: 2	5	6	7	7
Heavy Metals						
Lead (ppm)	≤ 0.2	AOAC 18th Edition: 2006 by ICPMS	0.108	0.0938	0.137	0.135
Arsenic (ppm)	≤ 0.5		0.300	0.270	0.252	0.252
Cadmium (ppm)	≤ 0.2		<0.0100	0.0112	0.0176	0.0186
Mercury (ppm)	≤ 0.05		<0.0100	<0.0100	<0.0100	<0.0100

Microbials						
Standard Plate Count (cfu/g)	≤ 50,000		8000	8200	8500	8200
Yeast and Mold (cfu/g)	Not more than 100		30	25	30	30
Coloforms (Enterobacteriaceae) (/25g)	Negative	Bacteriological Analytical manual 8th Edn, AOAC, USFDA, 1995.	Negative	Negative	Negative	Negative
E. Coli (/25g)	Negative		Negative	Negative	Negative	Negative
Salmonella (/25g)	Negative		Negative	Negative	Negative	Negative
Staphylococci (/25g)	Negative		Negative	Negative	Negative	Negative
Algal Toxin						
Microcystin (ppb/3g—DL: 0.5 ppb)	Not Detectable	Lawrence Et Al,: Journal of AOAC International Vol. 84, No.4, 2001	Complies	Complies	Complies	Complies

b. Residual Pesticide and Other Contaminant Analysis

Routine analysis of Certified Organic Spirulina powder for pesticides, aflatoxins, ochratoxin A, polycyclic aromatic hydrocarbons (PAHs), polychlorinated biphenyls (PCBs) and organochlorine and organophosphorous pesticides is carried out once per year. A random sample is sent to accredited laboratories identified by Parry. The compounds tested for by SGS laboratory in the three batches reviewed for this notification (batch numbers PS-0004-CNK/11-12, PS-0005-CNK/11-12 and PS-0006-CNK/11-12) include:

- Aflatoxins B1, B2, G1 and G2 (AOAC 18th edition 2006 using HPLC—detection limit 0.5–1.0 ppb)

- Ochratoxin A (AOAC 18th edition 2006—detection limit 2.5 ppb)

- Polyaromatic hydrocarbons (solvent extraction using GC/MS—detection limit 0.01 mg/kg)

- Polychlorinated biphenyl (AOAC 18th edition 2006 using GC-MS/LC-MS MS—detection limit 0.01 mg/kg)

- Organochlorine pesticides (AOAC 18th edition 2006 by GC-MS/LC-MS MS—detection limit 0.01 mg/kg)

- Organophosphorous pesticides (AOAC 18th edition 2006 by GC-MS/LC-MS MS—detection limit 0.01 mg/kg)

All compounds tested for, in all batches reviewed, were either not detectable or fell below the limits of detection for the specified assay.

c. Algal Toxins and Pheophorbides

To date, there is no report of any cyanobacterial toxins above specified limits in *Arthrospira* species, and their discovery is considered very unlikely to occur during monoculture of Spirulina in properly controlled and managed systems (Gershwin *et al.* 2008). It is true that some cyanobacteria can produce hepatotoxins or neurotoxins. For example, *Microcystis aeruginosa* produces microcystins, which are potent hepatotoxins and probable tumor promoters. Health Canada surveyed *Aphanizomenon flos-aquae* blue-green algal products from Upper Klamath Lake in southern Oregon to determine levels of microcystins and detected microcystins in 85 of 87 samples tested, with 63 samples (72%) containing concentrations of > 1 µg/g, the regulatory limit established by the Oregon Health Division and the Oregon Department of Agriculture (Gilroy *et al.* 2000). Despite the fact that *A. platensis* is not considered a toxigenic cyanobacteria species and that cultivation occurs in controlled ponds rather than natural lakes, Parry routinely tests finished products for microcystins and **has never detected** this toxin.

Pheophorbides are phototoxic chlorophyll catabolites formed when a chlorophyll molecule loses its magnesium atom and phytol residue, which occurs with acidity and chlorphyllase activity. It is associated in humans with photosensitive dermatitis (Endo *et al.* 1982). Although no cases of Spirulina-induced photodermatitis have ever been reported or published, Parry Nutraceuticals routinely tests finished Organic Spirulina Powder for the presence of existing and total pheophorbides (see Table 3). Total pheophorbides are calculated in the same way as existing pheophorbides are calculated, with the addition of a three-hour incubation period to promote the conversion.

d.   Shelf-life Stability

An accelerated nine-month shelf-life stability study was performed to assess the stability of Certified Organic Spirulina. Key parameters tested were moisture, total carotenoids, beta-carotene, xanthophylls, crude phycocyanin, and chlorophyll-a. Microbial parameters were also tested and consisted of yeast and mold, and a standard plate count. Tests were conducted monthly on batch number C602-NNK. Storage temperature was held at $40° \pm 2°$ Celsius and relative humidity was maintained at $75\% \pm 5\%$. Analytical methods applied and specifications used were those used for routine batch release. No adverse changes in stability were observed for the 9-month period and all parameters tested met the specifications at all time points, indicating Certified Organic Spirulina Powder is stable at 40° Celsius and 75% relative humidity for 9 months. Because this was an accelerated study, it was concluded that the product is likely to be stable for a period of three years under the recommended storage conditions.

Additionally, a real-time shelf-life study was performed, beginning July 2009. The ingredient was stored in a food grade aluminum pouch with N2 flushing, inside a box with stretch wrapping and tied with pop tape—stored at ambient temperature. The last measurement was performed on April 2011 (after 36 months). The sample will continue to be tested to determine the ultimate shelf-life. After 36 months, parameters including moisture, total carotenoids (mg/100g), beta carotene (mg/100 g), crude phycocyanin (%), chlorophyll a (%), standard plate microbial count and yeast and mold (cfu/g) still fell within specifications for the product. Xanthophyll levels (mg/100 g) decreased just slightly below specifications; measuring 249.8 mg/100 g after 12 months (specification 250–470 mg/100 g) and 243.9 mg/100 g after 36 months. This particular batch began with a xanthophyll level on the low end of the specification at the baseline measurement (252.7 mg/100 g), and some analytical variation is expected during the testing process. Additionally, 100 g is much higher than the expected serving size; hence the slightly decreased measurement on this larger scale would reflect a minimal change at the serving size level.

4. Self-limiting Levels of Use

There are no specific self-limiting levels of use for Certified Organic Spirulina.

5. Safety Assessment

(i) Toxicology Studies

GRN 000127, which was filed by FDA without questions, presents a detailed discussion of animal and human safety studies establishing quality and safety standards for Spirulina. In animals, safety evaluations involving acute, subchronic, chronic, mutagenic, teratogenic, carcinogenic, and multiple generation effects have been conducted over the last three decades. Both short- and long-term toxicity evaluations from various institutions around the world using different Spirulina samples demonstrate absence of toxicity in animals. A large number of human studies that utilized Spirulina are reported in the literature, a number of which indirectly attest to its safety.

The majority of toxicology studies in the literature on Spirulina were recently reviewed by Spirulina researcher and toxicologist Dr. German Chamorro of the National School of Biological Sciences, National Polytechnic Institute, México (Gershwin *et al.* 2008). In the 1970s and 1980s, Dr. Chamorro led comprehensive Spirulina animal studies sponsored by the United Nations Industrial Development Organization (UNIDO). Subchronic toxicity, chronic toxicity, effects on reproduction and lactation, teratogenicity, and mutagenicity were studied (Chamorro-Cevallos 1980). The results of these studies, along with some additional toxicology studies performed over the last twenty-five years, are summarized here.

a. Sub-Chronic Oral Toxicity Studies

The objective of the UNIDO-sponsored subchronic study was to detect any possible toxicity at Spirulina levels beyond the 10% of the diet that had been used in a previous study by Till and Willems in 1971 (Chamorro-Cevallos 1980). Levels of 20% and 30% were used in order to detect any toxicity at these higher percentages. Wistar rats were fed a diet of 10, 20, and 30% Spirulina (species not identified) in place of soy for a period of 13 weeks. Two control groups consisted of a soy-based diet group and a group fed a commercial diet commonly used in the laboratory. The five total groups each had 10 male and 10 female rats. Chamorro concluded that Spirulina fed to Wistar rats for three months at levels of 10, 20, and 30% in the diet did not affect any of the parameters studied, including weight, behavior, appearance, food consumption, hematologic or urologic parameters, GOT, GPT, alkaline phosphatase, and macroscopic and histopathological organ changes. No statistically significant changes occurred in any of the parameters with the exception of the relative weights of the seminal vesicles of animals treated with 20 and 30% Spirulina. Chamorro concluded that this was not of toxicological interest because there were no pathological findings during histopathological examination (Chamorro-Cevallos 1980).

Other subchronic studies using different feed preparations, administration times, and types of analyses have collectively found that Spirulina, even in high concentrations, produced no adverse effects (Gershwin *et al.* 2008). In a subchronic toxicity study in mice, *A. maxima* up to high feeding levels did not produce adverse effects after 13 weeks of treatment. Groups of 10 mice of each sex were given *S. maxima* in the diet at concentrations of 0 (control), 10, 20 or 30% for 13 weeks. The Spirulina had no effect on behavior, food and water intake, growth or survival. Terminal values in hematology and clinical chemistry did not reveal differences between treated and control groups. Post-mortem examination revealed no differences in gross or microscopic findings (Salazar *et al.* 1998).

GRN 000127 describes other independent feeding tests in France, Italy, Mexico, Japan, and India conducted during the 1970's and 1980's showing no undesirable results or toxic side effects.

b.   Chronic Oral Toxicity Studies

The objective of the UNIDO-sponsored tests for chronic toxicity, including functional tests, was to study the effects of large-scale Spirulina administration on hematological parameters, kidney function, serum chemistry parameters, and the weight and histopathology of certain organs. As in the sub-chronic study, Wistar rats were fed a diet of 10, 20, and 30% Spirulina in place of soy for a period of 80 weeks. Two control groups consisted of a soy-based diet group and a group fed a commercial diet commonly used in the laboratory. Each of the five total groups had 20 male and 20 female rats. Chamorro concluded that Spirulina did not produce any toxic effects in any of the parameters studied – weight gain, hematological parameters, liver and kidney function, terminal serum chemistry, mortality, relative organ weights, or histopathological parameters including tissue lesions and tumor incidence (Chamorro-Cevallos 1980).

Other chronic oral toxicity tests performed on rats to assess the cumulative toxicity of Spirulina also indicate no long-term effects on normal physiological or biological processes. For example, Wistar rats fed Spirulina at the maximum protein portion (14.25%) for 75 weeks showed no obvious signs of toxicity. Throughout the 18 months, the male animals fed the Spirulina diet showed weight increase comparable to the control animals fed a casein-based diet; the females fed Spirulina showed a slight decrease in weight up to the 30th week. Weight increases were comparable and a normal frequency of tumors occurred. No obvious signs of toxicity were observed. The authors concluded there was no evidence of toxicity related to the use of Spirulina as the sole source of protein in the rat (Boudene *et al.* 1975).

Other chronic toxicity studies were cited in Chamorro's recent review, including a 100-day study by Bourges et al in 1971, in which Chamorro reports that rats tolerated well a Spirulina-rich diet with a final concentration of 36% and 48%

protein. According to Chamorro, no histological abnormalities were found in several organs examined (Gershwin *et al.* 2008).

A 6-month oral toxicity study was performed on C57BL/6J mice using *Spirulina plantensis* in the diet at 0, 2.5 and 5% (*n*=8). Throughout the study, there were no signs of illness or behavioral changes in the mice, nor were there differences in body weight gain. Plasma AST levels were increased 2-fold in control male and female mice compared to baseline; this parameter was significantly lower in *S. platensis*-treated male mice after six months as compared to controls, and there was a trend toward a decrease in female mice as well. One hypothesis as to why this occurred is that the Spirulina may have prevented age-related tissue damage. There were no significant differences in liver histopathology compared to controls (Yang *et al.* 2011).

c.   Reproductive and Developmental Toxicity Study

To detect any consequences of feeding Spirulina to successive generations, an UNIDO-sponsored multigenerational study on reproduction and lactation was spread over a two-year period (three generations in approximately two years) and was completed in the last generation by a conventional sub-chronic toxicity study (Chamorro-Cevallos 1980). Wistar rats were divided into five groups of five males and five females each, and the groups were fed the same diets as for the chronic toxicity study. Fertility, gestation, lactation, and viability indices were recorded. For the 13-week sub-chronic part of the reproduction study, 10 males and 10 females were randomly selected from the F3b generation and general condition, weight increase, consumption and conversion efficiency, hematology, serum and urine analyses, and weight and histopathological examination of the organs were performed.

In the first generation, the fertility index was similar in all groups, and no negative effects of Spirulina in regard to terminations were observed. No modifications were observed in the viability or lactation indices of the litters. Mean weights of the litters matched the controls. Results corresponding to the second mating of this generation were reduced in relation to results of the first matings but were similar to controls, and the litter weights of this generation were similar to the controls. The lactation index for this group was slightly reduced compared to the first mating, but the litter growth during weaning was the same for the Spirulina and control groups. The results of the second mating of the F1b generation and the F2b generation showed no variations between the groups. Overall, no effects on fertility, litter size, or mortality were observed.

The results of the 13-week subchronic study performed on the third generation groups found significant differences in the male 20% Spirulina group, and in the female control group. Significant differences were also noted in the weights of the hearts, kidneys, and seminal vesicles of the males in the treatment groups and in the weights of the lungs and spleens of some females in the treatment groups. The differences were not dose-dependent and were not accompanied by pathological differences that could be attributed to Spirulina toxicity. Macroscopic examination revealed hydronephrosis in all groups, but no histopathologically examined lesions were attributed to Spirulina.

In other reproductive toxicity studies undertaken since Chamorro's and mentioned in his recent review, no developmental abnormalities have been observed at any time between zygote formation and postnatal maturation in Spirulina-fed rats, mice or hamsters (Chamorro-Cevallos 1980). In one additional study, *A. maxima* consumption had no effects on reproduction and peri- and postnatal development. At levels of 0, 10, 20 and 30% *A. maxima* incorporated into the diet, there was no reduction in body weight gain in males or females and no deaths or clinical signs of toxicity. Treatment was not associated with any adverse effect on any measure of reproductive performance, including male and female fertility and duration of gestation (Salazar *et al.* 1996).

The objective of the UNIDO-sponsored teratogenicity studies was to detect any spirulina-related embryonic resorptions or fetal malformations (Chamorro-Cevallos 1980). Wistar rats, CD-1 mice, and Dorado hamsters born to mothers fed 10, 20, and 30% Spirulina (species not identified) diets were used, along with two groups of controls as in the previous UNIDO-sponsored experiments. The Spirulina was fed to the treatment groups over three different periods during gestation. After the pregnant animals were weighed and sacrificed, fetuses of the sacrificed animals were counted, weighed, and examined for internal (visceral and skeletal) or external malformations; uterine wall implantations were counted to determine embryonic resorptions. From the data, a mean teratogenic index was calculated using the average percentages of control and treated animals affected. Some isolated cases of statistical significance occurred in the mean weight of the fetus, the number of implantations per fertile female, and the number of fetuses per pregnant female, but they did not show any relationship to the level of Spirulina fed to the animals. Chamorro's overall conclusion was that Spirulina does not cause gestational changes indicated by malformations, anomalies, or resorptions (Gershwin *et al.* 2008).

Teratogenicity was also examined in Salazar's study, mentioned above, in which *A. maxima* was administered in the diet of Wistar rats at the levels of 10, 20 and 30%. Spirulina-fed rats were mated and a portion of the pregnant rats was allowed to give birth. Development of the pups was monitored for viability, weight, and attainment of developmental markers. A portion of the pups was reared to maturity and reproductive performance was assessed. None of the measures of reproductive performance, including fertility and gestation duration, were associated with any negative effects. Nor were there increases in the number of abnormal pups or adverse effects on developmental markers or reproductive performance in the F1 generation (Salazar *et al.* 1996).

(ii) Additional Scientific Studies

While Spirulina has been consumed for hundreds of years in the diet, a number of human clinical trials performed in recent years further support safety of oral administration of Spirulina by confirming the absence of adverse effects. GRN 000127 presents a detailed discussion of various human studies that used Spirulina as the test article. Some additional human studies reporting no adverse effects are summarized here:

- A randomized, double-blind, placebo-controlled cross-over study of Spirulina in overweight adults was conducted by the Institut für Chemische Pflanzenphysiologie der Universität in Tübingen, Germany. The study consisted of 15 overweight patients with a mean age of 35.8 years and a mean BMI of 30.5 ± 5.2. Intake of 2.8 g Spirulina three times per day (8.4 grams total per day) for 4 weeks was associated with no adverse effects on blood pressure, heart rate, CBC, blood chemistry panel, kidney function, enzyme activities, or physical symptoms (Becker *et al.* 1986).

- A government-sponsored one-year feeding program with 5,000 rural pre-school children in India showed a decrease in Bitot's spots (a symptom of Vitamin A deficiency) from 80% to 10% after consumption of 1 g Spirulina per day for at least 150 days. The Spirulina was incorporated into noodles sweetened with sugar to preserve the beta-carotene. Called "Spiru-Om", it was well accepted by the children. The study was conducted by the Shri Amm Murugappa Chettiar Research Center in Madras, India.

- To evaluate the effects of Spirulina, sixteen males and 20 females, all healthy adults, orally consumed 4.5 grams Spirulina per day (3 tablets of 0.5 grams every 8 hours) for six weeks. At the beginning of the study and every week, fasting blood samples were taken and glucose, TAG, TC, HDL-C, and AST levels were determined to assess the potential hepatotoxic effects of treatment. No changes were observed in AST and glucose values throughout the experimental period (35 ± 18 UI/L and 85 ± 13 mg/dL respectively. No adverse effects were reported and the study authors reported that safety of oral administration was demonstrated (Torres-Duran *et al.* 2007).

- Thirty men with cardiovascular disease risk factors were fed Spirulina in addition to their normal diet. Group A consumed 4.2 grams daily for eight weeks. Group B consumed Spirulina for four weeks and were observed for another four weeks. Fasting blood samples were collected and WBC, GOT, GPT, LDH, gamma-GTP, alkaline phosphatase, uric acid, BUN, and creatine were measured at weeks 0, 2, 4, 6, and 8. No significant changes occurred in any of these parameters. No adverse effects were reported by any of the subjects and no problems were found on clinical examination (Nakaya *et al.* 1988).

- Seventy-eight subjects, aged 60–87 years, were given either 8 grams per day of Spirulina or placebo for four months in a randomized double blind study. The authors concluded that Spirulina is a suitable functional food for the elderly, and consumption resulted in favorable effects on blood lipids, immune variables and antioxidant capacity (Park *et al.* 2008).

- Children were fed 10–15 grams per day as a dietary supplement mixed with millet, water and spices, resulting in recovery from malnourishment within several weeks {Habib, 2008 #62859}.

- A search of clinicaltrials.gov outlines studies that evaluate oral consumption of 5 to 19 grams of Spirulina daily in various populations, suggesting that these levels are considered safe for use in those populations (trial numbers NCT00680277, NCT01141777, NCT01084382, NCT01195077).

(iii) History of Consumption

According to numerous historical records, Spirulina has been a component of the everyday diet of certain human populations for hundreds of years. For instance, it is generally agreed that the blue-green algae gathered from Lake Texcoco by the ancient Aztecs, made into dried cakes called *tecuitlatl* and regularly consumed in the diet, was indeed *Arthrospira* (Johnston 1970) (Deng *et al.* 2010). Bernal Díaz del Castillo first described this food during the Spanish conquests led by Cortes. While exact quantities of *tecuitlatl* consumed are unrecorded, daily consumption appears to have been the norm. A similar food, called *dihé*, was prepared from Spirulina gathered by the Kanembu tribes from alkaline lakes near Lake Chad in central Africa. First described in 1940 by the French phycologist Dangeard, *dihé*, composed almost exclusively from *A. platensis*, is used to make soups and sauces to accompany millet, and is still regularly consumed by the local populations near Lake Chad (Ciferri 1983; Habib *et al.* 2008). Based on surveys in Chad, frequency of consumption varies from one to six meals out of ten, and between nine and thirteen grams of spirulina are consumed per person during a meal (Delpeuch *et al.* 1975). Detailed accounts of the historical human consumption of other species of blue-green algae, including *Nostoc flagelliforme*, *Phylloderma sacrum*, and *Prasiola japonica*, also appear in the literature (Johnston 1970).

Commercial Spirulina production began in the 1970's. Today, *A. platensis* is one of the most commercialized micro algae, being cultivated for mass production for use in human food, animal feed, and colorimetric industry (Kim *et al.* 2007). It has been sold both in the United States and around the world since the late 1970s as a food product and dietary supplement. More than 3,000 tons of *A. platensis* are produced annually worldwide, and the majority is used for health food products and animal feed additives (Eriksen 2008). Some of the products found currently in the marketplace are listed below in section 5(v).

(iv) Previous Sales and Reported Adverse Events

Parry Nutraceuticals' Organic Spirulina Powder is currently sold in the United States as a dietary supplement, as well as both a dietary supplement and a food ingredient in other parts of the world. Since the year 1996, Parry Nutraceuticals has sold 1600 metric tons of Spirulina for use as dietary supplements, and has received no reports of serious adverse events.

To the best of our knowledge the FDA has not issued any letters regarding concern for safety to companies that market products containing *Arthrospira platensis* or any other *Arthrospira* species.

(v) Similar Products in the Marketplace

Spirulina is commercially available in a number of food and dietary supplement products as exemplified in Table 4 below:

Table 4: Commercially Available Food Products Containing *Spirulina*

Manufacturer	Product	Description	Label Claim
Betty Lou's, Inc. (USA)	Spirulina Ginseng Nut Butter Balls	Energy bar (ball)	1000 mg Spirulina
Raw Indulgence (USA)	Raw Revolution Organic Live Food Bars, Spirulina and Cashew	Raw food bar	Amount not listed
Lydia's Organics (USA)	Spirulina Bar	Raw food bar	Amount not listed
Freeland Foods (USA)	Spirulina Energy Bar	Raw food bar	Amount not listed
Rédei (Hungary)	Organic Spirulina spelt wheat pasta	Dried pasta	Amount not listed
Agisko (UK)	Spirulina pasta	Dried pasta	Amount not listed
K. Rogers Food Industries Sdn. Bhd. (Malaysia)	Spirulina and Cereal Butter Cookies & Spirulina Almond Cookies	Cookies	Amount not listed
Nature's Plus (USA)	SPIRU-TEIN® Bars, Wafers, Shakes, Ready-to-Drink	Protein bars, Protein powders, Protein wafers, Protein drinks	Amount not listed
Odwalla (USA)	Superfood	Green drink	1500 mg Spirulina
Odwalla (USA)	Superfood ™	Energy bar	500 mg Spirulina
Bolthouse Farms (USA)	Green Goodness	Green drink	Amount not listed
Naked Juice (USA)	Green Machine	Green drink	1300 mg Spirulina
Sambazon (USA)	Supergreens Revolution	Green drink	Amount not listed
Nutraceutical Sciences Institute	Spirulina	Powder to be added to water or juice	Suggested use: take 7000 mg spirulina one or more times daily
Earthrise	Spirulina Natural	Powder to be added to water or juice	Suggested use: take 3000 mg 1–2 times daily

(vi) Current Regulatory Status

An *Arthrospira platensis (A. platensis)* powder was the subject of a previous GRAS determination, submitted on behalf of Cyanotech Corporation and Earthrise Nutritionals, Inc. On the basis of scientific procedures, these two companies determined their spray-dried Spirulina powder is GRAS when used as an ingredient in foods such as bars, powdered nutritional drink mixes, popcorn, and as a condiment in salads and pasta, at levels ranging from 0.5 to 3 grams per serving size. FDA responded on October 6, 2003, having no questions regarding the notifiers' conclusion that Spirulina is GRAS under the intended conditions.

Since Parry Nutraceuticals' Certified Organic Spirulina is bioidentical to the subject of the previous notification, and because Parry Nutraceuticals follows the same raceway pond method of manufacturing, this GRAS determination incorporates by reference GRN 000127.

The Convention for the Use of Food Micro-Algae, Intergovernmental Institutional Spirulina Program (CISRI-ISP/ IIMSAM) works to promote the use of Spirulina against severe malnutrition. It has been established through two international agreements that are recognized in the UN Treaty Series. IIMSAM is accredited as a Permanent Observer Mission with the United Nations Economic and Social Council. It was also recommended as one of the primary foods during long-term space missions by both the National Aeronautics and Space Administration (NASA) and the European Space Agency (ESA) (Deng *et al.* 2010) (Habib *et al.* 2008).

Clinical studies in India and Africa have shown that, when Spirulina is used as a food complement, there is a significant response in the improved nutritional status of undernourished children (Simpore *et al.* 2006). The European Commission's Humanitarian Aid department (ECHO) funds supplemental feeding programs for about 65,000 Sri Lankan war refugees. The project funds *A. platensis* farming as the main food source of a low budget, high nutrition diet.

Antenna Technology is a Swiss-based organization composed of scientists and researchers working on issues of malnutrition by introducing Spirulina as a tool to fight child malnutrition. Antenna's publication, *The Nutritional Aspects of Spirulina* cites a study at Hôpital Bichat, France, of malnourished children and adults who were given doses of 80–90 grams Spirulina per day. Absorption of Spirulina proteins was found to be good, and despite these very large doses, no noteworthy increase in blood uric acid was demonstrated. The original publication verifying this reference could not be obtained (Falquet 1996).

Shri AMM Murugappa Chettiar Research Centre (MCRC), Chennai, India is a non-Governmental Voluntary Research Organization established in 1977. The MCRC trains rural people especially women to grow Spirulina for nutrition and income generation. They conducted the 18-month trial with 5,000 pre-school children listed under "Clinical Trials" above.

The Food and Agriculture Organization of the United Nations considers Spirulina to have significantly high macro- and micronutrient content, and discusses its important use as human food in its 2008 document entitled "A Review on Culture, Production and Use of Spirulina as a Food for Humans and Feeds for Domestic Animals and Fish" (Habib *et al.* 2008).

(vii) Information that may appear to be Inconsistent with GRAS Determination

Spirulina is considered safe for human consumption based on its long history of use as a food source, as well as numerous animal and human studies that demonstrate no safety concerns. There have been rare adverse incidences that have coincided with consumption of Spirulina supplements, although Spirulina causation has not been proven. A single case study was reported concerning a 28-year-old man who developed rhabdomyolysis after taking Spirulina for one month. He reported that he was not taking other supplements or medications and had no other risk factors (Mazokopakis *et al.* 2008). In contrast, a small clinical study showed potential preventive effects of exercise-induced skeletal damage (Lu *et al.* 2006). Another single case study was published of a 52-year-old Japanese man who showed signs of hepatotoxicity after taking Spirulina, although he was also taking three other medications. The signs resolved after discontinuation of the Spirulina and all medications (Iwasa *et al.* 2002). Lastly, a single case study reported an allergic reaction to Spirulina (specifically the phycocyanin component) by a 14-year old boy (Petrus *et al.* 2010). The reaction was confirmed by a positive prick test and oral challenge.

6. Intended Use

(i) Categories of Food

For the purpose of this GRAS self-affirmation, Parry Nutraceutical's Certified Organic Spirulina, manufactured in accordance with Good Manufacturing Practice (GMP) as specified in 21 CFR 110, is intended to be used as an ingredient in the categories of food discussed below.

Parry Nutraceutical's Certified Organic Spirulina is not intended for use in infant formula; or in meat, egg or catfish products, which would require additional review by USDA. Parry Nutraceutical's Certified Organic Spirulina is not intended for use as a color additive as per 21 CFR 70.3 (f), although like cherries, green or red peppers, chocolate and orange juice, it contributes its own natural color when mixed with other foods. As per 21 CFR 70.3 (g), it will be used in a way that any color imparted is clearly unimportant insofar as the appearance, value, marketability or consumer acceptability is concerned, and hence is exempt from FDA premarket approval requirements for color additives.

Parry Nutraceutical's Certified Organic Spirulina may be added to the following category of foods as defined in 21 CFR §170.3(n):

> (3) Beverages and beverage bases, nonalcoholic, including only special or spiced teas, soft drinks, coffee substitutes, and fruit and vegetable flavored gelatin drinks.

> (4) Breakfast cereals, including ready-to-eat and instant and regular hot cereals.

(16) Fresh fruits and fruit juices, including only raw fruits, citrus, melons, and berries, and home-prepared "ades" and punches made therefrom.

(20) Frozen dairy desserts and mixes, including ice cream, ice milks, sherbets, and other frozen dairy desserts and specialties.

(23) Grain products and pastas, including macaroni and noodle products, rice dishes, and frozen multicourse meals, without meat or vegetables.

(31) Milk products, including flavored milks and milk drinks, dry milks, toppings, snack dips, spreads, weight control milk beverages, and other milk origin products.

(33) Plant protein products, including the National Academy of Sciences/National Research Council "reconstituted vegetable protein" category, and meat, poultry, and fish substitutes, analogs, and extender products made from plant proteins.

(35) Processed fruits and fruit juices, including all commercially processed fruits, citrus, berries, and mixtures; salads, juices and juice punches, concentrates, dilutions, "ades", and drink substitutes made therefrom.

(36) Processed vegetables and vegetable juices, including all commercially processed vegetables, vegetable dishes, frozen multicourse vegetable meals, and vegetable juices and blends.

(37) Snack foods, including chips, pretzels, and other novelty snacks.

(38) Soft candy, including candy bars, chocolates, fudge, mints, and other chewy or nougat candies.

(40) Soups and soup mixes, including commercially prepared meat, fish, poultry, vegetable, and combination soups and soup mixes. This excludes foods that fall under USDA jurisdiction, such as;
- Catfish (USDA proposed rule 76FR10434)
- Soups that include more than "relatively small portions" meat and poultry within the products. Relatively small portions are as defined by 9 CFR 381.15 and the 2005 USDA Food Standards and Labeling Policy Book: 3 percent or less raw meat; less than 2 percent cooked meat or other portions of the carcass; or 30 percent or less fat, tallow or meat extract, alone or in combination. In the case of poultry, less than 2 percent cooked poultry meat; less than 10 percent cooked poultry skins, giblets or fat, separately; or less than 10 percent cooked poultry skins, giblets, fat and poultry meat (limited to less than 2 percent) in any combination.
- Soups that include more than "relatively small proportions" of egg (as defined in 9 CFR 590.5 (h), p. 660 under subtitle "Egg product".

(ii) Estimated Daily Intake (EDI)—Exposure

In FDA GRAS notification No. 127 (submitted by Cyanotech Corporation and Earthrise Nutritionals, Inc.), which FDA filed with no questions, the Spirulina addition level was stated as 0.5 to 3 grams per serving. A high-end consumer was estimated to potentially consume 6 grams of Spirulina per day; a medium consumer was estimated to consume 3 grams per day, and a low-end consumer was estimated to consume a maximum of 12 grams per month. The Spirulina in the present GRAS notification is the same species of Spirulina as in GRAS notification 127, and uses a similar manufacturing process. Cyanotech Corporation and Earthrise Nutritionals, Inc. stated heavy metal specifications in their notification; < 0.05 ppm for mercury, < 0.5 ppm for cadmium, < 1.0 ppm for lead, and < 1.0 ppm for arsenic. The heavy metal specifications of Parry Nutraceutical's Organic Spirulina are the same and/or more conservative as compared to those in the Cyanotech and Earthrise notification, and are as follows; < 0.05 ppm for mercury, < 0.2 ppm for cadmium, < 0.2 ppm for lead, and < 0.5 ppm for arsenic.

Organizations around the world generally encourage consumption of Spirulina rather than limit it, especially in populations that are malnourished {Habib, 2008 #62859}. To calculate an estimated daily intake (estimated exposure) for Certified Organic Spirulina, a USDA Nutrition Insights article (a publication of the USDA Center for Nutrition Policy and Promotion)—Insight 20 October 2000 (Basiotis *et al.* 2000) is referenced. According to this publication, males aged 51 or greater consume the greatest number of servings of food per day. They consume an average of 18.2 total servings of food per day from the following food groups: grains, fruits, vegetables, milk, meat and other (fats, oils, sweets). According to the same publication, the smallest number of total daily servings of food is that consumed by females aged 19–24, who consume 12.5 total servings per day. Because Certified Organic Spirulina is intended for use in foods categories that span all of these food groups, it is reasonable to consider this data when calculating the estimated daily intake of Spirulina.

For the purpose of this GRAS notification, using the above referenced USDA data, the estimated number of total food servings per day for a high-end consumer would be 18.2 (males aged 51 or greater). The number of total servings consumed by females aged 19–24 (12.5 servings per day) was used for calculations to represent a low-end user. If one quarter of a person's daily food intake contained Certified Organic Spirulina at the same addition levels as specified in FDA GRAS No. 127 (0.5–3 grams per serving) and using the USDA figures for the minimum and maximum number of servings of food consumed in the US, the resulting daily exposure would range from 2.28–13.7 g/day.

7. General Recognition

The scientific studies performed in both animals and humans that provide the basis of this GRAS determination by scientific procedures, and information related to the historical consumption of Spirulina which corroborates the scientific safety data, are published and available in the public domain. The reference section of this notification contains the citations for these published studies. This published data, along with government positions that promote the use of Spirulina as a food, provide ample evidence of consensus among qualified experts that there is reasonable certainty that consumption of Certified Organic Spirulina is not harmful. The general availability of this information satisfies the common knowledge component of this GRAS notification.

8. Basis for the GRAS Determination

Based on an independent and collective critical evaluation of the data and information described above, the Expert Panel, qualified by scientific training and experience to evaluate the safety of substances added to food, concluded that Parry Nutraceutical's Certified Organic Spirulina, when produced according to Good Manufacturing Practice and meeting the specifications presented in this notification, is generally recognized as safe for its intended use based on scientific procedures, and is hence exempt from the requirement of premarket approval. The previous FDA GRAS notification No. 127 for Spirulina, which was filed by FDA without question, was taken into account for this determination, as were the numerous toxicological studies performed on Spirulina. A plethora of publications in the public domain, including human and animal studies, demonstrate that there is common knowledge and consensus among qualified experts that Spirulina is safe for its intended use. The safety and quality control data that are the basis of the safety evaluation are corroborated by the long and extensive history of safe consumption of Spirulina by humans worldwide.

9. References

Amin A, Hamza AA, Daoud S, *et al.* Spirulina protects against cadmium-induced hepatotoxicity in rats. *American Journal of Pharmacology and Toxicology.* 2006; 1: 21-25.

Basiotis P, Lino M and Dinkins J "Consumption of Food Group Servings: People's Perceptions vs. Reality." Nutrition Insights 20, 1-2. 2000.

Becker EW, Jakover B, Luft D, *et al.* Clinical and biochemical evaluations of the alga Spirulina with regard to its application in the treatment of obesity: a double blind cross-over study. *Nutr Rep Int.* 1986; 33: 565-574.

Boudene C, Collas E and Jenkins C. [Determination of various toxic minerals in spiruline algae of different origins, and evaluation of long-term toxicity in the rat of a lot of spiruline algae of Mexican origin]. *Ann Nutr Aliment.* 1975; 29: 577-588.

Chamorro-Cevallos G. Toxicological Studies on Spirulina Alga Sosa Texcoco S.A. Pilot Plant for the Production of Protein from Spirulina Alga, United Nations Industrial Development Organization; 1980.

Chamorro-Cevallos G, Garduno-Siciliano L, Barron BL, *et al.* Chemoprotective effect of Spirulina (Arthrospira) against cyclophosphamide-induced mutagenicity in mice. *Food Chem Toxicol.* 2008; 46: 567-574.

Ciferri O. Spirulina, the edible microorganism. *Microbiol Rev.* 1983; 47: 551-578.

Delpeuch F, Joseph A and Cavelier C. [Consumption and nutritional contribution of the blue algae (Oscillatoria platensis) among some populations of Kanem (Tchad)]. *Ann Nutr Aliment.* 1975; 29: 497-516.

Deng R and Chow TJ. Hypolipidemic, antioxidant, and antiinflammatory activities of microalgae Spirulina. *Cardiovasc Ther.* 2010; 28: e33-45.

Desikachary IV and Bai NJ. Taxonomic studies in Spirulina II. The identification of Arthrospira ("Spirulina") strains and natural samples of different geographical origins. *Algological Studies.* 1996; 83: 163-178.

Devi MA and Venkataraman LV. Hypocholesterolemic effect of blue green algae Spirula platensis in albino rats. *Nutrition reports international.* 1983; 28: 519-531.

Endo H, Hosoya H, Koyama T, *et al.* Isolation of 10-Hydroxypheophorbide a as a Photosensitizing Pigment from Alcohol-treated Chlorella Cells. *Agricultural and Biological Chemistry.* 1982; 46: 2183-2193.

Eriksen NT. Production of phycocyanin--a pigment with applications in biology, biotechnology, foods and medicine. *Appl Microbiol Biotechnol.* 2008; 80: 1-14.

Falquet J. Spiruline, Aspects nutritionnels. *Publicaciones Antenna Technology.* 1996.

Garrity GM. Bergey's Manual of Systematic Bacteriology: Springer; 2005

Gershwin ME and Belay A, Eds. Spirulina in Human Nutrition and Health. Boca Raton: CRC Press; 2008.

Gilroy DJ, Kauffman KW, Hall RA, *et al.* Assessing potential health risks from microcystin toxins in blue-green algae dietary supplements. *Environ Health Perspect.* 2000; 108: 435-439.

Habib M and Parvin M. A review on culture, production and use of spirulina as food for humans and feeds for domestic animals and fish. FAO Fisheries and Aquaculture Circular No. 1034. Rome, Food and Agriculture Organization of the United Nations (FAO); 2008: 1-41.

Iwasa M, Yamamoto M, Tanaka Y, *et al.* Spirulina-associated hepatotoxicity. *Am J Gastroenterol.* 2002; 97: 3212-3213.

Jensen GS, Ginsber DI and Drapeau C. Blue-green algae as an immuno-enhancer and biomodulator. *Journal of the American Nutraceutical Association.* 2001; 3: 24-30.

Johnston HW. The biological and economic importance of algae, Part 3: Edible algae of fresh and brackish waters. *Tuatara.* 1970; 18: 19–35.

Khan Z, Bhadouria P and Bisen PS. Nutritional and therapeutic potential of Spirulina. *Curr Pharm Biotechnol.* 2005; 6: 373-379.

Kim CJ, Jung YH and Oh HM. Factors indicating culture status during cultivation of Spirulina (Arthrospira) platensis. *J Microbiol.* 2007; 45: 122-127.

Lee JB, Srisomporn P, Hayashi K, *et al.* Effects of structural modification of calcium spirulan, a sulfated polysaccharide from Spirulina platensis, on antiviral activity. *Chem Pharm Bull (Tokyo).* 2001; 49: 108-110.

Lu HK, Hsieh CC, Hsu JJ, *et al.* Preventive effects of Spirulina platensis on skeletal muscle damage under exercise-induced oxidative stress. *Eur J Appl Physiol.* 2006; 98: 220-226.

Mazokopakis EE, Karefilakis CM, Tsartsalis AN, *et al.* Acute rhabdomyolysis caused by Spirulina (Arthrospira platensis). *Phytomedicine.* 2008; 15: 525-527.

Nakaya N, Homma Y and Goto Y. Cholesterol lowering effect of Spirulina. *Nutr. Rep. Int.* 1988; 37: 1329-1337.

Park HJ, Lee YJ, Ryu HK, *et al.* A randomized double-blind, placebo-controlled study to establish the effects of spirulina in elderly Koreans. *Ann Nutr Metab.* 2008; 52: 322-328.

Petrus M, Culerrier R, Campistron M, *et al.* First case report of anaphylaxis to spirulin: identification of phycocyanin as responsible allergen. *Allergy.* 2010; 65: 924-925.

Reddy CM, Bhat VB, Kiranmai G, *et al.* Selective inhibition of cyclooxygenase-2 by C-phycocyanin, a biliprotein from Spirulina platensis. *Biochem Biophys Res Commun.* 2000; 277: 599-603.

Romay C and Gonzalez R. Phycocyanin is an antioxidant protector of human erythrocytes against lysis by peroxyl radicals. *J Pharm Pharmacol.* 2000; 52: 367-368.

Salazar M, Chamorro GA, Salazar S, *et al.* Effect of Spirulina maxima consumption on reproduction and peri- and postnatal development in rats. *Food Chem Toxicol.* 1996; 34: 353-359.

Salazar M, Martinez E, Madrigal E, *et al.* Subchronic toxicity study in mice fed Spirulina maxima. *J Ethnopharmacol.* 1998; 62: 235-241.

Scheldeman P, Baurain D, Bouhy R, *et al.* Arthrospira ('Spirulina') strains from four continents are resolved into only two clusters, based on amplified ribosomal DNA restriction analysis of the internally transcribed spacer. *FEMS Microbiol Lett.* 1999; 172: 213-222.

Simpore J, Kabore F, Zongo F, *et al.* Nutrition rehabilitation of undernourished children utilizing Spiruline and Misola. *Nutr J.* 2006; 5: 3.

Tomaselli L, Palandri MR and Tredici MR. On the correct use of the Spirulina designation. *Algological Studies.* 1996; 83: 539-548.

Torres-Duran PV, Ferreira-Hermosillo A and Juarez-Oropeza MA. Antihyperlipemic and antihypertensive effects of Spirulina maxima in an open sample of Mexican population: a preliminary report. *Lipids Health Dis.* 2007; 6: 33.

Upasani CD and Balaraman R. Effect of vitamin E, vitamin C and spirulina on the levels of membrane bound enzymes and lipids in some organs of rats exposed to lead. *Indian Journal of Pharmacology.* 2001; 33: 185-191.

Vonshak A, Ed. Spirulina platensis (Arthrospira): Physiology, Cell-biology and Biotechnology. Bristol, PA: Taylor & Francis; 1997.

Yang Y, Park Y, Cassada DA, *et al.* In vitro and in vivo safety assessment of edible blue-green algae, Nostoc commune var. sphaeroides Kutzing and Spirulina plantensis. *Food Chem Toxicol.* 2011.

LETTER OF PROPOSAL

Wai Kit Chiang
At
IIMSAM Executive Office
211 E 43rd St. Suite 2300
New York, NY 10017
wkc@iimsam.org

17 April 2011

Dear Sir:

Nutrient is the primary fuel in the human body. It provides the needed materials for reproduction and development. If the body encounters difficulties and requires restoring and improving the body, nutrient is the primary source of medicine and health improvement.

In a cybernetic and mechanically developed age of man, much power and energy source will be required. Should anything happen to a power source, power plant or power production area, another source of power for energy source and power will be needed.

In a community and organization, power is in strength by support and joint effort. Communication enables this strength. Should anything occur causing effect on the community and organization this strength must be restored. To restore and retain encouragement, material power and nutrient fuel for the organism body must be maintained.

If the need for the amount of nutrient is greater than the amount of nutrition (food) the body can consume and hold, food is a luxury. If power for the community is greater than the gifts of power can provide, power plants will have to be built. If the social economic structure of the community is greater than the given capitals can provide, the economic society will have to assist the devastated community back into the society to trade and communicate with others.

Economy is the primary means of trading resource within the world of man. All members in the autonomous body of mankind must restore world economy, a factor in the infrastructure of mankind. All who can assist in restoring damages in the damaged organization would do best through an organized plan of operation. Different parties will have something different to contribute for the benefit of the damaged society. Let a meeting between the executor(s) of the damaged community be held with the super health nutrient manufacturers, power production companies and the economical organizations of the world.

Let the efforts toward Japan, Haiti and others who are trying to restore from difficulties be samples of success for this plan of operation. It is suggested that the party that is offering proposal for the meeting between executor(s) of the damaged communities, the food manufacturing companies, the power manufacturing companies, and the economic society, to mediate in the meetings.

From

Wai Kit Chiang, MNCM
Senior Advisor to the Chief of Administrative & Protocol Affairs
Executive Office Manager & Technical Research

REFERENCES

1. Bowerman, O'Connell, Orris & Porter. *"Essentials of Business Statistics: Second Edition."* McGraw-hill. Copyright@2008.

2. *Carr-Snyder. "Management Information Systems: Voice/VoIP Administration with lab". McGraw Hill/Irwin. Copyright@2007.*

3. Fitzgerald, Jerry, Dennis, Alan. *"Business Communications and Networking, 9th Edition".* John Wiley & Sons. Copyright@2007.

4. Gates, Jr., S. James. *"Superstring Theory: The DNA of Reality".* The Teaching Company. Copyright@2006.

5. Gazzaniga, Michael S., Ivry, Richard B., Mangun, George R., *"Cognitive Neuroscience: The Biology of the Mind, 3rd Ed".* W.W. Norton & Company. Copyright@2009.

6. Greenberge, K. Hentschel, Weinert, F. *"Compendium of Quantum Physics".* Springer Publishers. Copyright@2009.

7. Held, Gilbert. *"Ethernet Network's 4th Ed.".* John Wiley and Sons, LTD. Copyright@2003.

8. Jenkins, Gail W., Kemnitz, Christopher, Tortora, Gerald, J. *"Anatomy and Physiology from Science to Life".* John Wiley & Sons. Copyright@.

9. Kaeo, Marke. *"Designing Network Security, 2nd Ed".* Cisco Press. Copyright@2004

10. Moskowitz, Clara. *"Strange Particles May Travel Faster Than Light, Breaking Laws Of Physics."* LiveScience. Copyright@22 Sept. 2011.

http://news.yahoo.com/strange-particles-may-travel-faster-light-breaking-laws-192010201.html.

11. Moskowitz, Clara. *"Long-Sought 'God Particle' Cornered, Scientists Say"*. LiveScience. Copyright@14 Dec. 2011. http://news.yahoo.com/long-sought-god-particle-cornered-scientists-140202981.html.

12. *Natural News, "Discover the radiation protective benefits of Spirulina and Chlorella",* http://www.naturalnews.com/031779_spirulina_radiation.html.

13. Pfleeger, Sharles P., Pfleeger, Shari Lawrence. *"Security in Computing, 4th Ed"*. Pearson Education, Inc. Copyright@2007.

14. Potter, Ned. *"Neutrino Faster Than Light...Maybe. Revising Relativity?"* ABC Science. Copyright 23 Sept. 2011. Web Sight http://abcnews.go.com/blogs/technology/2011/09/neutrino-faster-than-light-maybe/.

15. Restak, Richard, MD, Bechtel, Stefen, Daniels, Patricia, Hitchcock, Susan Tyler, Gura, Trisha, PhD, Stein, Lisa, Thompson, John, *"Body: The Complete Human"*. National Geographical Society. Copyright@2007.

16. Schumacher, Benjamin. *"Quantum Mechanics: The Physics of Microscopic World"*. The Teaching Company. Copyright@2009.

17. Shames, Irving M. *"Engineering Mechanics: Statistics & Dynamics, 3rd Ed"*. Prentice-Hill. Copyright@1980.

18. Spohn – Brown – Grau, *"Computer Science: Data Network Design, 4th Ed"*. McGraw-Hill Companies, Inc. Copyright@2008.

19. Spirulina Benefits: *"The Health Benefits of Spirulina"*, http://www.spirulina-benefits-health.com/spirulina_health_benefits.html.

20. Sweeney, Michaels. Forwarded by Restak, Richard, MD. *"Brain the Complete Mind"*. National Geographic. Copyright@2009.

21. *Sapolsky, Robert. "Biology and Human Behaviour: The Neurological Origins of Individuality, 2nd Ed." The Teaching Company. Copyright@2005.*

22. Singh, Anuradha, MD. *"100 Questions & Answers About Epilepsy".* Jones and Bartlett Publishers, Inc. Copyright@2006.

23. *Sun Tzu. "The Art of War: Translated from the Chinese by Lionel Giles". Dover Publication, Inc. Copyright@2002.*

24. Toigo, Williams Jon. Forwards by Shannon, Michael and Ferris, Gregory. *"Disaster Recovery Planning: Preparing for the Unthinkable, 3rd Ed".* Prentice Hall PTR. Copyright@2003.

25. Techrepublic, *"OSI"*; http://search.techrepublic.com.com/search/OSI.html

26. Techrepublic, *"Storage Area Network"*; http://search.techrepublic.com.com/index.php?q=storage+area+network

27. Techrepublic, *"TCP"*; http://search.techrepublic.com.com/index.php?q=TCP

28. Techrepublic, *"Telecommunications"*; http://search.techrepublic.com.com/search/Telecommunications.html

29. Wikipedia, *"Cloud computing"*, http://en.wikipedia.org/wiki/Cloud_Computing

30. Wikipedia, *"Internet Protocol"*; http://en.wikipedia.org/wiki/Internetwork_protocol IP; http://search.techrepublic.com.com/index.php?q=IP

31. Wikipedia, *"Network Hardware"*; http://search.techrepublic.com.com/index.php?q=network+hardware

32. Wikipedia, *"Talk: Wireless"*; http://en.wikipedia.org/wiki/Talk_Wireless

33. Wikipedia, *"Router"*; http://en.wikipedia.org/wiki/router.

34. Wikipedia, *"Wireless"*; http://en.wikipedia.org/wiki/Wireless_communication

35. Wikipedia, *"Human Brain"*, http://en.wikipedia.org/wiki/Human_brain.

36. Wikipedia, *"Central Nervous System"*, http://en.wikipedia.org/wiki/Central_nervous_system.

37. Wikipedia, *"Nervous System"*, http://en.wikipedia.org/wiki/Neural_system.

38. Wikipedia, *"Neural Network"*, http://en.wikipedia.org/wiki/Neural_network.

39. Wikipedia, *"Hormone"*, http://en.wikipedia.org/wiki/Hormones.

40. Wikipedia, *"Methyl Group"*, http://en.wikipedia.org/wiki/Methyl.

41. Wikipedia, *"Amino Acid"*, http://en.wikipedia.org/wiki/Amino_Acid.

42. Wikipedia, *"Organism"*, http://en.wikipedia.org/wiki/Organism.

43. Wikipedia, *"Metabolism"*, http://en.wikipedia.org/wiki/Metabolism.

44. Wikipedia, *"String Theory"*, http://en.wikipedia.org/wiki/String_Theory.

45. Wikipedia, *"Energy Level"*, http://en.wikipedia.org/wiki/Energy_level.

46. Wikipedia, *"Organic Chemistry"*, http://en.wikipedia.org/wiki/Organic_chemistry.

47. Wikipedia, *"Protein"*, http://en.wikipedia.org/wiki/Protein.

48. Wikipedia, *"Nucleic Acid"*, http://en.wikipedia.org/wiki/Nucleic_acid.

49. Wikipedia, *"Cell (Biology)"*, http://en.wikipedia.org/wiki/Cell_%28biology%29.

50. Wikipedia, *"Gene"*, http://en.wikipedia.org/wiki/Genes.

51. Wikipedia, *"Factor VII"*, http://en.wikipedia.org/wiki/Factor_VII_deficiency.

52. Wikipedia, *"Hemophilia"*, http://en.wikipedia.org/wiki/Factor_VIII_deficiency.

53. Wikipedia, *"Chernobyl"*, http://en.wikipedia.org/wiki/Chernobyl_disaster.

54. Wikipedia, *"Centripetal Force"*, http://en.wikipedia.org/wiki/Centripetal_force.

55. Wikipedia, *"Blood Vessel"*, http://en.wikipedia.org/wiki/Blood_vessel.

56. Wikipedia, *"Neuron"*, http://en.wikipedia.org/wiki/Neuron.

57. Wikipedia, *"Carbon"*, http://en.wikipedia.org/wiki/Carbon.

58. Wikipedia, *"Special Relativity"*, http://en.wikipedia.org/wiki/Special_relativity.

59. Wikipedia, *"Spirulina (dietary supplement)"*, http://en.wikipedia.org/wiki/Spirulina_%28dietary_supplement%29.

60. Wikipedia, *"Nutrition"*, http://en.wikipedia.org/wiki/Nutrition.

61. Wikipedia, *"Nutrient"*, http://en.wikipedia.org/wiki/Nutrient.

62. Wikipedia, *"Dietary Supplement"*, http://en.wikipedia.org/wiki/Food_supplement.

63. Wikipedia, *"Firehall"*, http://en.wikipedia.org/wiki/Firehall.

64. Wikipedia, *"D.A.R.Y.L."*, http://en.wikipedia.org/wiki/DARYL.

65. Wikipedia, *"In the Womb"*, http://en.wikipedia.org/wiki/In_the_Womb.

66. Wikipedia, *"The Art of War"*, http://en.wikipedia.org/wiki/The_Art_of_War.

67. Wikipedia, *"Neutrino"*, http://en.wikipedia.org/wiki/Neutrino#Mass.

68. Wikipedia, *"Lepton"*, http://en.wikipedia.org/wiki/Lepton.

69. Wikipedia, *"Capital"*, http://en.wikipedia.org/wiki/Capital.

70. Wikipedia, *"Trade Credit"*, http://en.wikipedia.org/wiki/Trade_credit.

71. Wikipedia, *"Free Trade"*, http://en.wikipedia.org/wiki/Freetrade.

72. *Wilson, Richard. "Einstein's Relativity and the Quantum Revolution: Modern Physics for Non-Scientists, 2nd Ed." The Teaching Company. Copyright@2000.*